ABOU

I write sexy romances. I us ...nder *xleglover* and *Flash of Stocking* on various sites.

My stories are romances, so they explore the feelings, emotions and relationships of the characters. My stories have an emotional edge to them. The characters have thrilling adventures, but there's pain there too, at least for some of them.

I try to write stories that seem like real life. Yes, the situations are extreme, but I hope you come away thinking, "*Yes, I can see how that might happened.*"

You can find my books at *Amazon Kindle* and *Smashwords*. Also, *Barnes & Noble, Apple Books,* and *Rakuten kobo*. If you'd like to join my mailing list or would like to send me a question or feedback, please email me at *peteandrews1701@gmail.com.*

BOOKS BY PETE ANDREWS

Faithful Wife's Fall From Grace (on-going series)

Book 1
Book 2
Book 3
Book 4

Girls Who Belong To Other Men (2 book series)

Book 1
Book 2

Opening Pandora's Box (5 book series)

Book 1: Jessie Plays For Her Husband
Book 2: Ollie Watches His Wife With Another Man
Book 3: Jessie Grows Closer To Roman
Book 4: Jessie Loses Herself In Roman
Book 5: How Can You Do This To Me?

Available at Amazon Kindle and Smashwords.

CHAPTER 1

Ollie moved towards the bedroom. Staggered really, as he was still recovering from Jessie's punches to his gut from moments ago. He knew they weren't intentional. Jessie was either oblivious to how her words and actions hurt him, or she thought she was pushing his buttons to excite him.

And it was true his fantasies were a conflict of lust and emotions. What got him excited also pained his heart. So Ollie knew it wasn't Jessie's fault. She was just doing what he'd been asking – *cajoling*—her to do for years. Yes, their game had turned from fantasy to reality. But he was the one who pushed her into all this.

Ollie heard Jessie moan again. And there was the conflict. Her moan at what another man was doing to her was a dagger into his heart, but also turbo fueled his cock. He was already hard again, even though he'd cum just moments ago.

As he neared the bedroom, Ollie realized he was naked from the waist down. He thought that looked stupid, so he tugged off his shirt. Then he saw himself in the bathroom's full length mirror (the bathroom was across from the bedroom).

He looked at himself. He imagined what Jessie saw when she looked at him. An average height, somewhat cute, slim white guy. Mostly hairless except for the hair on his head. With a below average cock.

Then Ollie imagined what his wife saw when she looked at Roman. Very handsome and tall, with a dark Mediterranean complexion. Broad shoulders, ripped chest, muscular arms and legs, six pack abs. Close shaven beard, hair on his chest and arms. Huge cock. On top of all that, he was an excellent lover who knew his way around a woman's body.

Feeling both disheartened and extremely turned on, Ollie walked into the bedroom.

Jessie was on her back with Roman on top of her. She was still wearing the lingerie from before, although the Louboutin high heels with the red soles were now scattered on the floor.

Jessie's legs were open wide, and Roman (who was naked) was fucking her. He was taking long, slow strokes into her womanhood.

Roman was fucking Jessie in the bed they shared. Their *marital* bed.

Jessie getting fucked in their marital bed by another man was so powerful to Ollie. He'd known it would be, but seeing the reality of it happening right in front of him was crushing to his soul. To his manhood. Yet, his cock was so incredibly hard.

Jessie's head was on her pillow. But her sexy ass was propped up on his. On *his* pillow. The pillow he put his head on at night. Another man was fucking his wife on his pillow. And that man was getting his pillow wet with his and Jessie's sex juices.

The sight was so wrong. *Jessie let Roman put his pillow there?* Ollie wondered. He felt betrayed. And he knew they'd fucked in their marital bed before. Did they use his pillow that way before? The prospect was so – fucking – delicious. There was the conflict again. Ollie hated it. But part of him hoped Jessie told Roman to do it. Part of him hoped she told Roman, *"Put my husband's pillow under my ass so you can fuck me better."*

Ollie shivered at these thoughts. He ached at these thoughts.

As Roman fucked her, he lightly kissed Jessie's lips, her cheeks, her neck, and behind her ear. Jessie especially responded whenever Roman's lips touched behind her ear. Ollie knew that was a sensitive spot for her. He wondered if she told Roman about it, or if he figured it out himself. Ollie didn't know which was worse.

Jessie's beautiful face was strained, and her body was tense. Her eyes were clenched shut. Her arms were tightly wrapped around Roman's neck, and her nails were digging hard into his back. Her pretty lips were set in the shape of a grimace, and what came out were constant, soulful moans.

Ollie wasn't sure if she was in the throes of cumming. But if it was an orgasm, it was the longest he'd ever seen. Could this be the g-spot orgasm she'd told him about?

Finally Jessie's face and body relaxed. She loosened her grip on Roman. And her moans turned to heavy breathing.

"That was so freaking amazing," she panted. "I can't believe how you make me cum that hard, and long."

Roman responded by kissing her softly. Then he put Jessie's long, shapely legs on his shoulders, and he began fucking her harder and faster.

Roman pushed down hard so the front of her thighs pressed against her bra-covered tits. The lovers kissed and panted into each other's mouth as Roman relentlessly fucked Jessie's pussy.

"Yeah, yeah, fuck me Roman, fuck me," Jessie changed as he pounded her.

Roman had amazing strength and staying power. After what had to be over 10 minutes of intense, hard fucking, Jessie cried out "Oh god Roman! I'm cumming again!"

Ollie was awestruck. She was cumming again? Already?

Roman never stopped fucking her hard, even as her tight, sexy body lurched and bucked with her climax. Finally after minutes more of hard fucking, Roman growled "I'm cumming! Where do you want it?"

"Inside me! Cum inside me!" Jessie cried.

Roman pounded into her hard, ejaculating his virile seed with each thrust. Then finally they were done.

Ollie watched as they did the dance of carefully pulling out, like before. Then Roman collapsed onto his back, next to Jessie. The condom was still on his softening cock. The top reservoir was full of his milky sperm.

Jessie rolled over to him and pressed her little slim body into his. Roman wrapped his arms around her. Jessie wrapped her arm and one of her stockinged legs around him, hugging her pretty face into his muscular chest.

At that moment, they looked like more than lovers. They looked like they were a couple. They looked like they were in love.

The sight was too much for Ollie. He left the bedroom. He found a t-shirt and boxers and put them on. Then he poured himself a scotch and sat in the chair in the TV room. He waited.

How long until she comes out to me? he asked himself.

Maybe she's forgotten I'm here. Maybe they'll go at it again, and she won't come out to me for an hour. Two hours.

Then the worst thing sprung into Ollie's mind. *Maybe she'll ask me to let Roman spend the night. Let him sleep in our bed. With me on one side of her, and him on the other. Maybe I'll wake up in the middle of the night, with Roman fucking Jessie again right next to me. No, not fucking. Making love to her.*

But as these dark thoughts flitted through Ollie's head, Jessie came out of the bedroom. Gone was the lingerie. She was wearing what she often wore to bed, one of his old Penn State t-shirts.

Ollie prepared himself for the worst. For Jessie to say *"Hey Ollie, it's late. Can Roman sleep over?"*

But instead, Jessie didn't say anything. She climbed into Ollie's lap, wrapped her arms around his neck, and snuggled her head into his shoulder.

Moments later, Roman emerged from the bedroom. He quickly gathered his clothes and got dressed.

"See you, Ollie. It was fun," Roman said. Ollie nodded at him.

"See you later Jessie," he said.

Jessie didn't move. With her face still pressed into the crook of Ollie's neck, she softly said "See you."

Roman nodded at both of them, and a moment later he was gone.

CHAPTER 2

Once Roman was gone, Jessie looked up at her husband. "Are you okay?" she asked.

"It was kind of hard watching sometimes," Ollie admitted. He forced a grin onto his face. "I know you've been together a few times ...."

"Four times," Jessie said.

"Yeah," Ollie said. "But this was only the second time I've watched you with him. And this time it was in our bed."

"Our marital bed," Jessie said. She knew that was what it was called in *Literotica* stories. And that other website Ollie liked, *ourhotwives*. She knew the impact *martial bed* had on Ollie.

And it did have an impact on Ollie. He felt a punch to his gut – and a surge in his loins – as she said it.

"It got you hot though, right?" Jessie asked. She reached between their bodies and felt his cock through the boxers. "You're so freaking hard, Ollie."

Ollie gasped at her touch. He pushed his boxers down and adjusted Jessie on his lap. She wasn't wearing panties under his old Penn State t-shirt.

"Roman fucked you hard," he said. "Are you sore?"

"Yeah."

"I'll be gentle," Ollie said as he guided his cock into his wife's pussy.

"I know you will baby," Jessie said.

Ollie paused and pulled back slightly to look at her. Was that a slight? A criticism that he didn't fuck her hard and rough like Roman?

Reading his thoughts, Jessie said "I want you to be gentle." She kissed him softly. "That's who you are. That's why I love you." She kissed him again.

Ollie forced himself to believe his wife. Anyway, he wasn't able to think about it now. At that moment, he needed release. He needed to fuck Jessie. To reclaim her as his wife.

Ollie groaned as he entered Jessie. "Fuck you're so loose!" he gasped. His cock felt almost no pressure from her normally tight pussy walls.

"Yeah, yeah," Jessie panted as she rode her husband's cock. "Roman stretched me so much Ollie," she said, pushing her husband's buttons. "He ruined my pussy for you, baby."

Ollie's jaw dropped, remembering his thoughts from the other night when he was alone in the hotel room. He had wondered to himself how long it would take for Roman's big cock to ruin Jessie's pussy for him.

Jessie saw his expression and said, "Does that get you hot baby?" She kissed Ollie as she moved up and down on his shaft. As she did, she squeezed her pussy walls so she felt tighter around his cock. "Do you feel that baby? I can still do that, make my pussy tight for you. But if I keep fucking Roman, I might not be able to do that anymore. He'll stretch me so much you won't be able to feel anything when we're fucking. Does that turn you on baby? Do you want that to happen?"

"Jessie, Jessie," Ollie groaned. He hugged his wife tight as she stroked his cock with her pussy. Moments later he came.

Ollie continued to hold Jessie tight against him as his cock softened and fell out of her. Then they moved to their bedroom. Jessie arranged them so Ollie wasn't in the wet spot. She handed Ollie his pillow but he said "He fucked you on that."

"Oh ... sorry," Jessie said. She gave him her pillow. She thought about using Ollie's pillow for herself but thought better of it. She reached over and grabbed another pillow. Then they pressed their bodies together and hugged each other.

They were silent for long moments as they held each other. Finally, Ollie asked "Did you use my pillow on purpose?"

Jessie knew her husband's questions were a big deal for him. It was part of what he got out of their game. "Honestly I don't remember how it got there. I think he just put it there."

"So he did it on purpose?" Ollie said, his tone more accusing than he intended.

Jessie kissed her husband, and gently said "Baby, I don't think Roman knows which pillow is yours and mine."

Ollie nodded. He said "I watched you in our bed. Before and after. And it looked like he really means something to you."

Jessie answered cautiously, feeling like she was on dangerous ground. "I thought that was okay? You know, the *it's just a crush* thing?"

"Yeah ...," Ollie said, the jealously and angst bearing down hard on him. "So you do feel something for him." It was both a statement and a question.

"Ollie baby," Jessie said, still speaking cautiously. "Didn't we talk about this already?"

"Yeah," he said, reluctantly agreeing.

Jessie looked into his face. She also reached between their bodies and felt his cock. "Baby, you look upset. But you're hard again already."

"I told you. It's—."

"It's the angst," Jessie finished for him.

"Yeah," Ollie said with a sheepish smile.

Jessie hugged him tighter. "It's okay baby," she assured him. "We're doing this together. It's our game."

"Yeah," Ollie good. It felt so incredibly good to hug his wife. With a crooked grin, he asked "So you had fun on your date with your boyfriend?"

Jessie laughed. "So he's my boyfriend now?" she asked with a grin.

"I guess we can call him your crush," Ollie joked.

Jessie laughed and said "Maybe he'll give me his high school ring to wear." As the words left her lips, she felt his cock jerked against her thigh. "Oh ... I guess I just found another one of your buttons," she said with a giggle.

Ollie grinned. "So you had fun with him?" he asked again.

"I did," Jessie admitted. "I mean, new relationships are fun. They're exciting."

"Jessie baby, he fucked you in the alley," Ollie said.

"Oh my god," Jessie said with a delighted glint in her pretty blue eyes. "He called it a *wall fuck*. I've never heard that before."

"Has anyone ever done you that way before?" Ollie asked.

"Done me? No," Jessie said with a laugh. Then she traced her fingertip across his mouth. "You can *do me* that way sometime."

"I don't think so," he said.

"Why?"

When he didn't answer immediately, she asked again, "Why Ollie?"

Looking a bit embarrassed, Ollie said "There are some positions that aren't as good for me."

Jessie didn't understand at first, but then she got it. With his smaller manhood, there were some positions where his penis couldn't penetrate her as well.

Now that she thought about it, in all their time together, Ollie had never taken her standing up, and rarely in the doggy position. Usually they did it missionary, or with her on top. She had always assumed Ollie liked those positions better because he was sweet and considerate, and he liked to make love instead of just fuck. But now she knew different.

"So you liked getting wall fucked?" Ollie asked.

"Yeah, I liked it," Jessie replied. "It was crazy. I could hear people talking on the street."

"You liked that? The risk they might see you?"

"I don't know ... maybe," Jessie said with a laugh.

"He was able to get deep inside you?" Ollie asked. He was beginning to breath harder.

"Yeah, so deep baby," Jessie said. She reached between their bodies and found his hard cock. She began stroking him. He moaned at her touch.

"Deeper than I get in you?" Ollie asked excitedly.

Jessie pulled Ollie on top of her. She opened her legs and guided his cock into her pussy.

Once Ollie was balls deep inside her, she said "Yeah, Roman was way deeper than you. He touches places you never get close to."

"Oh god Jess ...," Ollie moaned. He fondled her little perfect tits as he fucked her slow. "How did he know to kiss behind your ear?"

"What?"

"How did he know you like that? Did you tell him?"

"No. He figured it out," Jessie said. Then looking into her husband's fuck face, she added "It took you a long time to figure that out. Roman was a lot faster."

"So Roman's a better lover than me?" Ollie asked excitedly.

Jessie had already told Ollie that Roman was the best lover she'd ever had. But she knew these questions excited him. So she said "Yeah baby. Roman's better. He fucks me better than you."

"Oh fuck Jess!" Ollie cried as he came.

Ollie rolled off and lay next to Jessie. He was panting hard.
They were silent for long moments.

Jessie was tired and drifting off, when Ollie said, "We're fucking a lot."

"What?" she asked sleepily.

"You and me," Ollie said. "We're having sex a lot. And I'm cumming in you a lot. And you're not on the pill."

Not Jessie was awake. "So, is that a bad thing?" she asked. She'd gone off the pill as they were thinking about starting a family.

"I'm just saying, if you get pregnant, it'll stop our game," Ollie said.

"I guess I don't understand your point."

"I don't have a point," Ollie said with a shrug. "I don't know. I'm just kind of thinking out loud."

Jessie turned and got on an elbow to look at her husband. "Let's not over think it Ollie," she said. "If you get me pregnant, then maybe that's God saying we've had our kinky fun and now it's time to grow up."

Ollie got on his side and looked back at his wife. He said "Would you be disappointed? If you had to stop seeing Roman?"

Now Jessie understood what Ollie was getting at. He was worried that maybe she would choose Roman over him.

Jessie gently said, "I'm crushing on him, right? There's some infatuation going on. So yeah, I'd be disappointed. It would be like breaking up with him, and there's always emotions with breakups. But I'd get over it. Is that what you're worried about?"

"I guess I am," Ollie admitted.

Jessie gave him a kiss. She said, "It's okay, Ollie. I'd get over it. Over him. Okay baby?"

Ollie smiled as he said "Okay."

Then they snuggled together and fell asleep.

CHAPTER 3

Jessie was surprised when Alisha called out of the blue. "Do you want to grab coffee?" Alisha asked. "To catch up?"

"Ah, sure," Jessie said hesitantly. *Does she know about me and Roman?* she asked herself. "Starbucks?"

"God no," Alisha scoffed. "They brew swill. Let's do Culture Expresso. The one at Bryant Park."

"Okay," Jessie said, cringing at Alisha's judgmental attitude. With Alisha, it was always awkward. Although she didn't mind going to Culture Expresso. She loved their chocolate chip cookies.

Later that afternoon, Jessie walked into Culture Expresso. Alisha was already there. Jessie ordered a skinny latte and chocolate chip cookie, and then joined Alisha at her table.

"Not worried about your waistline?" Alisha said, looking at the cookie.

"Um ... I like the way they're warm," Jessie sputtered. "And anyways, I got a skinny."

"You look really good," Jessie said looking at Alisha. And she did. Her hair was styled. Her makeup perfect. She'd lost weight. And she was wearing a clinging dress that showed off her curves, especially her big boobs.

"I'm on the market again, so I have to look good," Alisha said.

"You don't think you'll get back together with Roman?" Jessie asked. She felt butterflies in her stomach as she waited for Alisha to answer.

"Not in a million years," Alisha said with finality.

Inside, Jessie was relieved, and her spirits soared. But instantly she chastised herself. She was married to Ollie, not Roman. Why should she care if Roman and Alisha got back together? In fact, she should *want* them to reconcile, at least for the children's sake. But still, Jessie couldn't help feeling happy that Roman and Alisha wouldn't be getting back together.

Then Alisha dropped the bombshell. She said, "You know he cheated on me."

Jessie's lips parted in shock. "He did?"

Alisha nodded. Looking disgusted, she spat out, "Roman's a mother fucker. Pardon my French. The best thing about him is his big dick. But he can't keep it in his pants. He thinks he's God's gift to women."

Jessie looked down at her feet. She didn't know what to say. And she was still processing this new information that Roman had cheated on Alisha.

Jessie had a visceral reaction to a husband cheating on his wife. Her father cheated on her mother, and it almost led to their divorce. She'd die if Ollie cheated on her.

"Anyway, whatever," Alisha said dismissively. "I've got a new man now."

"Your old boyfriend?" Jessie asked.

"What?" Alisha responded, not understanding.

"Um ... Roman said you moved in with your old boyfriend," Jessie said hesitantly.

"What, Chad?" Alisha said laughing. "He's a friend. I stayed with him a couple days. But he's not an old boyfriend. Chad's gay. Flaming in fact."

"Oh," Jessie said. She was silent, processing all this. *Roman cheated on Alisha, and he lied about who she was staying with,* she thought to herself.

"No, my new man isn't Chad," Alisha said, the laughter still in her voice. "Look," she said, extending her leg out from the table.

Jessie looked at Alisha's leg, not sure what she was supposed to be looking at. Then her eyes went wide. On her ankle, just above her high heel, was a Queen of Spades tattoo.

Alisha looked pleased with herself. "My new boyfriend's Jamal," she said. "I got this for him. He's black."

"Yeah, I, ah ..., I figured that," Jessie said, still staring at the QoS tat on Alisha's ankle.

"Sex is better with Jamal," Alisha said. "You know what they say about black men and how big they are? Well, it's true." She laughed.

"Jamal's dick is bigger than Roman's," Alisha said, continuing. "Which I admit is saying something since Roman's hung. And Jamal's not just bigger. He fucks better than Roman."

Jessie stared off into the space over Alisha's shoulder, feeling awkward and not knowing how to respond.

"Anyway, I want to ask you something," Alisha said, leaning over the table towards Jessie, like they were about to talk about secret stuff. "I heard Roman has a girlfriend. Do you know who it is? I don't care. We're over. I'm just curious."

"You heard a rumor?" Jessie said, alarms going off in her head.

"From Pastor John," Alisha said with a nod.

"*From Pastor John?*" Jessie gasped, her eyes going wide with shock.

Alisha nodded again. "Roman bragged to someone at church, and Pastor John heard about it," she said. "Roman can't keep his zipper shut, and he can't keep his mouth shut either. I just want to know who the slut is."

Jessie felt like the world was spiraling apart. She managed to sputter out, "I haven't heard anything."

Alisha eyed Jessie for long moments. "My kids say you're at my house a lot," she said.

"I've been trying to help," Jessie stammered nervously. "Help Roman with your kids. You know ... I bought some groceries and made a couple hot meals. To give Roman a break ...." Jessie knew she was talking too much. She probably sounded defensive. And guilty.

Again, Alisha eyed Jessie for long moments. Then she said, "That's very sweet of you."

"Well, anyway, you'll tell me if you find out who Roman is seeing?"

"Yes, of course," Jessie lied.

"By the way, how is Ollie?" Alisha asked.

"He's fine," Jessie said.

"He still travels a lot?" Alisha asked.

Jessie and Alisha looked at each other for a long moment. Jessie felt like Alisha was looking into her soul.

Then Jessie said, "Yes he does." Her head was spinning. And she was worried she looked guilty. She made an excuse about having to get back to work for a meeting, and rushed out of the café.

CHAPTER 4

J essie didn't go back to work. She went to Manhattan Motion, Roman's gym.

Being dressed for work, she knew she couldn't easily approach Roman. So she sought out Brooke, her dance instructor friend.

"Can you get Roman? I need to talk to him," Jessie whispered. The gym was crowded with the lunch workout crowd, and she didn't want to be overheard.

"Are you alright?" Brooke said, seeing the distress on Jessie's face. She knew about Jessie and Roman's affair.

"I'm just ... can you get him?" Jessie asked. She nervously looked around the crowded gym, trying to figure out a place they could talk in private.

Brooke read her thoughts. "Go to Roman's office," she whispered. "I'll tell Roman to meet you there."

"His office?"

"You know the hallway going to the tanning salon? The storage room off that hallway?" Brooke asked.

Jessie nodded yes.

"Roman has an office in the back of that storage room," Brooke told her. "Go there."

Jessie nodded. She began walking towards the hallway, trying to look as inconspicuous as possible. It was impossible though, not with her beautiful face and lush blonde hair, and her tight sexy body in the fitted dress and high heels she'd worn to work. All the men in the gym watched her as she walked towards the hallway.

Jessie didn't notice Roman when he entered his office. Her back was turned to him, as she was looking at the pictures hanging on the wall.

Roman paused a moment to look at his lover. He liked what he saw. Especially her sexy ass in that tight dress. And her long shapely legs in dark hose. And the shiny black high heels on her pretty feet. She was delicious eye candy. He figured the men in her office had perpetual hard-ons with her around. And for Roman, Jessie was more than eye candy. She was his fuck buddy.

"Hey sexy," he said to her.

Jessie turned to look at him. "Why do you have these pictures?" she asked, waving at the photos hanging on the wall behind his desk.

"They're from the grand opening," Roman said.

"They're all girls," Jessie pointed out.

"Not all of them," Roman said. Jessie scoffed. Most of the people in the pictures were girls. All young and pretty. All with big boobs. All with short dark hair.

"How many have you fucked?" Jessie asked accusingly.

"None of the dudes," Roman joked.

"How many?" Jessie pressed.

Roman frowned. "What is your problem today?" he said. He was starting to get annoyed and defensive.

"How many?" Jessie asked again.

"A few, okay?" Roman said, still frowning at her.

"How many before you broke up with Alisha?"

Roman's eyes narrowed. "What are you getting at?"

"Answer me," Jessie insisted. "How many did you fuck behind Alisha's back?"

"You should talk."

"Fuck you Roman," Jessie said angrily. "You know I'm not doing anything behind Ollie's back."

"Why does any of this matter to you? It's not like we're committed to each other or anything."

"That's right we're not committed. I'm married."

"Yeah, I know, and you throw that in my face all the time," Roman shot back. "You control everything. We talk when you say. We're together when you say. We fuck when you say. What kind of relationship is that?"

"How can we have a relationship? I'm *freaking—married—Roman*," Jessie said again, emphasizing each word like he was stupid. "We hook up sometimes. That's what we do. And why would I want to have a relationship with you anyways? When you cheat."

"How can I cheat on you?" Roman said, getting angry. "You're fucking married, right? So if I fuck Bianca or Fletcher or whoever, it's not cheating on you."

"You cheated on Alisha!" Jessie said angrily. "You cheated on your wife!"

"What are you talking about?"

"I saw Alisha today! She told me you cheated on her!"

"Why do you care if I cheated on Alisha?" Roman said, his voice rising with anger.

"Because it tells me the kind of man you are!" Jessie spat back. "And you lied to me! Alisha didn't move in with her old boyfriend! She told me Chad is gay!"

"What else did that bitch tell you?"

"She told me you're bragging at church about having a new girlfriend! And now Alisha thinks it's me! And maybe Pastor John thinks that too! Maybe Pastor John thinks I'm cheating on Ollie!"

"From what I've seen, you *should* be cheating on Metro Ollie," Roman said derisively.

Jessie moved close and slapped Roman across his face. "Don't you dare talk that way about him!" she said angrily. "He's a way better man than you! He doesn't cheat! He's not just a big dick like you! That's all you are! A dick!"

Roman glared with anger. He looked furious.

Jessie had never seen him like this. Roman was a big man, and he was enraged with anger. He stepped towards her and she felt afraid. But she didn't back away from him.

"Oh you love my big cock!" he snarled. "You cum really hard on my cock!"

"You wish I loved your cock!" Jessie spat back.

"We'll see about that!" Roman growled. He suddenly grabbed Jessie and twisted her around. He pushed her down so her breasts were pressed against his desk. He gripped both of her shoulders so she couldn't move.

"Roman no!" Jessie cried.

"Oh don't play the faithful wife. We know you're not that," Roman hissed into Jessie's ear as he jerked up her skirt.

"Roman stop," Jessie whined. She couldn't move and felt helpless. And she felt exposed with her skirt hiked up.

Then Roman pulled down her pantyhose and ripped off her thong, making her feel even more exposed and vulnerable. "Roman, please ..." she begged.

With his foot, Roman kicked her legs open. Jessie's high heels scraped across the concrete floor as he forced her thighs apart.

Roman reached to her front and fingered her pussy. She was wet.

"Don't play the victim. You want this. You love getting fucked," he taunted her.

"Let me go Roman!" Jessie cried.

"You want this," Roman said as he rubbed his fat cockhead between Jessie's pussy lips.

Jessie couldn't stop herself from moaning. Roman heard it and laughed triumphantly. "I know you want this," he said. He reached around her front and squeezed her breasts hard, so hard it made her yelp with pain. "I'm gonna give you what you want! What Metro Ollie can't!"

"Stop Roman," Jessie begged, tears welling up in her eyes.

"Admit I fuck you better than Ollie, and I'll let you go," Roman hissed into her ear. "Say *you fuck me better than Metro Ollie*, and I'll let you go."

"Just let me go Roman," Jessie whined.

"You had your chance," Roman said harshly. He took hold of his big hard cock and rammed it into Jessie's pussy.

"Oh god! It hurts! Stop!" Jessie cried. He had never penetrated her before so abruptly. So roughly. *It hurt!* Tears ran down her cheeks.

"It hurts so good, right Jessie?" Roman taunted as he forced more of his cock into her. He reached around her front and again groped her tits through her dress and bra. His hands were so big her little A cups easily fit in his palms. He found her nipples and squeezed them hard, making Jessie cry out in pain again.

"I know you Jessie! You love this!" he hissed into her ear.

"You don't know me!" Jessie cried.

"I know everything about you!" Roman said as he ravaged Jessie's pussy. "You play all innocent with your blue eyes and blonde hair. But you're not innocent. You show off your body, you tease. You wanna be used. You wanna be fucked. The way I wall fucked you. You loved that. You wanna be treated like a slut."

"Nooooo ....," Jessie whined as Roman roughly fucked her from behind.

But her body was betraying her. She gripped the edges of the desk with her sweet pink painted fingers as tendrils of pleasure circled her clit and spread through her body.

Jessie couldn't move with Roman's big body on top of her, and with her pussy impaled with his big cock. She was helpless, completely at his mercy. And he was taking advantage of her helplessness by abusing her body.

But Jessie knew she could still hurt him. Men like Roman were all ego. And she knew how to hurt his ego.

Through clenched teeth as he pounded her from behind, she hissed, "You know what else Alisha told me? Her new boyfriend's a black man. Jamal. She said Jamal's cock is bigger than yours. She said Jamal fucks better than you. She even got a tattoo for Jamal. Did Alisha ever do that for you Roman?"

Jessie's words enraged Roman even more. He took it out on her pussy, fucking her even harder and faster now, each violent thrust lifting Jessie out of her high heels and making the sharp points of the stiletto heels scrape against the floor.

"You bitch!" Roman growled, and he grabbed Jessie's blonde hair in a fist and jerked her head back. "Here's a present for your precious Ollie!" he hissed as he sucked hard on her neck, so hard it made her cry out with pain. He wanted to mark Jessie the way Jamal had marked Alisha!

Roman ran his tongue up her neck. Then he sloppily licked inside her ear.

Jessie groaned at the sensation. Normally she hated ear play because that part of her was too sensitive. But this time, it was like pulling the pin of a grenade. Suddenly, Jessie cried out as her body exploded in a massive orgasm.

Even as the orgasm reverberated through her body, Roman roughly flipped Jessie over so now her back was on his desk.

Roman forced Jessie's legs onto his shoulders as he continued to violently pound her. In this position, he was able to get even deeper inside her.

Roman was getting close. "I'm not wearing a condom!" he growled. "You hear me Jessie? I'm not wearing a condom!"

"Look at me Jessie!" he ordered her. "I want you looking at me when I cum inside your slutty pussy! Maybe I'll put a baby inside you the way Jamal put a tat on Alisha!"

Moments later, Roman growled as he came. He gripped her hips tight, and pushed in as deep as possible. He stayed that way as he orgasmed. Jessie looked into Roman's eyes as his virile seed sprayed her unprotected, fertile womb.

"Oh god!" Jessie groaned as she felt the powerful jets of his sperm splashing against her pussy walls. The sensations sent her over the edge and she came again. She cried out as orgasmic pleasure flooded her tight sexy body.

They looked at each other as they panted hard, their bodies tingling from their orgasms. Roman purposefully kept his cock inside Jessie, trapping his seed deep inside her fertile womb.

———◉———

Jessie sat on the sofa in Roman's office, covered by a blanket. She hugged her knees to her chest.

Roman pulled his desk chair over so he could sit facing her. "I did cheat on Alicia," he admitted. "About six months ago. We were practically not married anymore. We weren't talking. No intimacy. No sex. So one time I slipped up. It was a girl I met in a bar. I'm not saying this is an excuse. I'm just telling you what happened."

"I never cheated on her with Bianca or Fletcher, or any other girl," Roman said. "They came later, after me and Alisha were separated. I swear Jessie. It was just that one time."

Jessie nodded but didn't say anything. She seemed a million miles away.

"And yeah, I lied about Chad being her old boyfriend," Roman admitted. "I guess I wanted you to feel sorry for me."

Jessie still didn't say anything.

"And okay, yeah, I told some people at church I was seeing someone. That's it. I didn't say it was you. If Alisha or Pastor John or whoever thinks it's you, they figured it out themselves."

When Jessie still didn't respond, he said, "She probably doesn't know anything. She's just trying to turn you against me. She's throwing shit about me to all our friends. She's even saying she's going to try to get sole custody of the kids. I'll never see them."

Jessie's eyes went wide as, suddenly, she seemed to come back to life. She said, "But how can she? You're a better parent than her."

"I don't know," Roman said. He looked despondent, but encouraged she was at least talking. "My lawyer says that's how it is. Moms always come first. If Alisha gets her way, I'll only get to see the kids on weekends sometimes."

"I'm sorry Roman. I hope it works out," Jessie said. Then her voice trailed off, the wall between them coming up again.

After a few moments of silence, he said "So ... sorry about before. I was pretty rough. Sorry."

Jessie shrugged but didn't say anything. She seemed to hug her knees closer to her chest.

"Did I hurt you?" he asked.

"I'm fine," Jessie said. Then she moved to get up. "I better get going."

Roman grabbed her arm, gently this time. "Are we okay? When will I see you next?"

Jessie hesitated a moment. Then she said, "I'll call you."

CHAPTER 5

Later that evening, Jessie phoned Ollie. First she told him about her conversation with Alisha. Then she told him she had sex with Roman. He didn't wear a condom, and he came inside her.

"Do you think I should take a morning after pill?" Jessie asked.

Ollie felt lightheaded. His excitement was so intense, his body was on the verge of those uncontrollable shakes. He willed his voice not to shake as he said, "If you're pregnant, it could be mine. We had sex last night. And the night before too."

"That's true," Jessie said. "But Roman cums more than you."

Ollie shuddered inside. His wife's words were so terrible, yet so delicious too.

Again he forced himself to calm down. He said "It only takes one sperm. And he might cum more than me, but we have sex more." Then to lighten the mood, he joked "Not that this is a competition or anything."

Jessie gave a laugh. It was without humor though.

"So what does that mean?" she asked.

"We've talked about this," Ollie said. "This is a dangerous game we're playing. But a lot of the excitement is the danger."

"So we shouldn't do anything?"

"Maybe make him wear a condom next time," Ollie joked with a laugh.

Jessie hesitated. Then she said, "He was really rough today."

"What do you mean?"

Jessie described how Roman pinned her to the desk, pressing down hard so she couldn't move. She told him to stop, but he didn't. She'd felt helpless and powerless as he pulled up her skirt and fucked her from behind. She said how he flipped her around and told her to look into his eyes as he came.

"He didn't give me a chance to tell him to wear a condom," Jessie said. "I don't think he would've anyways."

Ollie was silent for long moments. He was breathing hard, both from excitement and anger.

"So he forced you?" he said angrily.

"Calm down baby," Jessie said soothingly. "I like it when Roman is rough with me."

Again Jessie's words were so horrible. She liked it when *Roman* was rough with her, but not him. Not her husband.

But Ollie had enough self-awareness to know he could never be rough with the Jessie, his wife, the girl he loved more than anything. She was too precious to him. And it wasn't his personality anyway – or physique—to treat any girl that way.

He was breathing hard when he asked, "So you liked it?"

"I'm not sure I'd say that," Jessie said. "I guess I'm still processing it all."

"Have you told him your fantasy?"

"No Ollie," Jessie replied. "I've only ever told you."

They were talking about Jessie's deepest, darkest sexual fantasy.

Jessie fantasized about forced sex. About a dominate man forcing himself on her.

In her fantasy, Jessie's helpless as the man uses her body for his own pleasure. The man doesn't care about Jessie as he fucks her. He doesn't care about her needs, or how she feels. But, as if out of spite, he forces her body to betray her.

And then he forces her to cum. That's the ultimate humiliation. Despite the horrors of being taken while helpless, of a man using her body without her permission, Jessie is forced to cum. The man forces her to orgasm.

"Did it ...," Ollie began. He found it hard to say the words. "Did it feel like he was raping you?"

"No it wasn't rape," she said immediately with certainty. "I'm sure he would've stopped if I told him to stop."

"You did tell him to stop."

"You know what I mean," Jessie said. "If I'd *really* told him to stop. If I yelled and screamed. Or fought back."

Ollie stared at Jessie for a long moment.

"And you came?" he eventually asked. "Roman forced you to cum?"

Jessie's insides shuddered at her husband's words. About being forced to cum.

She softly said, "First he, you know, worked my body. He was rough. He pushed me down on the desk so I couldn't move. Then he pulled up my skirt and forced my legs apart. He fucked me hard, and he squeezed my breasts. Really hard. It hurt. He even licked inside my ear. You know how I hate that. But it just added to everything. That's when I came. The first time he forced me to cum."

Jessie shivered as she re-lived the moment.

"He even – Ollie, you won't like this – he even sucked hard on my neck, and left a mark. That added to it too. Because you told him not to mark me, and he did it anyway."

Ollie tried to swallow but his throat was dry. He couldn't speak. He could barely breathe. His cock was so hard it hurt in his pants. But his heart was in turmoil too. Roman made Jessie's fantasy a reality. Not him, but another man.

"And then ...," Jessie continued. "He said he wasn't wearing a condom. And he was going to cum inside my slutty pussy. That's what he said. My slutty pussy."

"I was helpless. I couldn't stop him. And then he came. He came so hard I literally felt his cum hitting my walls."

"Ollie, it felt so amazing. It made me cum again."

"He kept his cock inside me. It was still mostly hard. Ollie, it was like the stories you read on the internet, where the bull is trying to keep his sperm inside the wife's pussy. Like he's trying to breed her."

"Oh god Jess ...," Ollie softly moaned.

"You know what he said Ollie? Before he came?"

"What?" Ollie asked breathlessly.

"He said, *maybe I'll put a baby inside you the way Jamal put a tat on Alisha.*"

"Oh god Jessie!" Ollie groaned. He wasn't touching himself, but she was going to make him cum in his pants.

"And I couldn't do anything," Jessie said. "Afterwards, I couldn't think, or say anything. I was numb."

"Ollie baby, was it like that for you?" Jessie asked. "The first time your fantasy became true? When I had sex with Roman the first time?"

Ollie was panting. Jessie was too, becoming aroused as she re-lived this with her husband.

For long moments, neither said anything. Only their heavy breathing could be heard over the phone.

"Yes," Ollie finally said. His voice was heavy and throaty with lust. "It was a journey. All the playing we did before Roman. Each time you were with someone, flirting, dancing, touching ... each time it happened, it took my breath away. But yeah, when you finally got together with Roman ... that night, when he kissed you, and got on your knees and took out his cock ...."

Ollie's voice trailed off. His heart was pounding as he remembered that night, and he was having a hard time breathing.

"And when you put his cock in your mouth," Ollie continued, his voice so low and throaty he was barely audible. "And then when he penetrated you ... when he was inside you with his cock ... when he made you cum. And when he came inside you ...."

Ollie's voice trailed off again. His body was shaking with excitement. He needed a moment to compose himself.

He finally said, "Yeah ... yeah ... it was really something. It was life changing."

The married husband and wife were silent again.

"Can I talk about something?" Ollie asked. "Change the subject?"

"Of course baby," Jessie said.

She heard a zipper opening and some shuffling. It told her Ollie was talking out his cock to stroke himself.

"Do you think Alisha really thinks it's you?" he asked.

"I don't know," Jessie said. "People see us together at church. People gossip. And Alisha said her kids tell her I'm over there sometimes. So I think she might suspect. And she did ask me if you still travel a lot."

"That gets me hot," Ollie said. "If she thinks you're having an affair with Roman, and cheating on me."

"What about the people at church? What about Pastor John?"

"That's hot too," Ollie admitted. "Especially if Pastor John thinks you're cheating on me. He's the senior pastor but you know he's not that old. Maybe early 40s. He'd probably like to get in your pants."

"God baby that's evil," Jessie bemoaned. "You know Pastor John is very conservative, right? He's celibate."

"I'm just kidding about Pastor John. And I wouldn't want people to find out for real," Ollie assured her. "I just like the idea that people are gossiping."

Jessie shook her head. She couldn't stand the thought of Ollie cheating on her. But wife cheating was part of Ollie's cuckold fantasies. She didn't understand it, but then she had wild fantasies too. So she wasn't going to judge her husband's sexual fantasies. And, she admitted to herself, because of his fantasies, she got the benefit of having sex with Roman.

"You didn't ask me before seeing Roman," Ollie said.

"I wasn't planning on fucking him," Jessie said.

"Are you sure?"

Jessie was about to answer that she was sure, but then she hesitated. If she was honest with herself, maybe she hoped they'd end up having sex. "I guess I'm not," she admitted. Then she gently asked, "But ... am I supposed to ask you first? I thought I'm his girlfriend."

Ollie's body seized up. He lustfully moaned into the phone, "God Jessie. The things you say."

He was stroking himself slow. He wanted to edge himself and make this last.

"You have to use condoms," Ollie told his wife. "Or make him pull out. But if things get out of control like today, and you get pregnant ... and who knows what'll happen, if Roman wants to breed you –."

Jessie cut him off, saying, "He didn't say that."

"He said he wants to put a baby inside you, the way Jamal tatted Alisha," Ollie reminder her. "And he got Alisha pregnant 3 times. Maybe that's his thing."

"It's how you say it," Jessie said. "*Breed*. It's like, pagan-ish. And if that's really what you think ... god Ollie, what are we doing?"

"It's part of the risk," Ollie said, trying to assure his wife that it was okay. "We both get off on the risk. The danger."

Jessie didn't reply. She didn't deny it.

"I'm just saying, if you do get pregnant, the baby's mine," Ollie said firmly. "Okay? You have to promise me."

"Ollie baby, of course, the baby will be yours," Jessie promised.

"You like when he's bareback inside you, and cums inside you, right?" Ollie asked.

When Jessie didn't answer, he pressed "You like that, right?"

Jessie hesitated another moment, then admitted, "Yes."

Then seeing how excited her husband was, she teased, "Maybe Roman does want to breed me."

"Oh god Jess!" Ollie moaned. He was so close to cumming.

"I want you to see him again," Ollie said, his words coming out like a moan. He was in major cuck-space now. "On a date. I want you to go on another date with your boyfriend."

"The last time, Roman said that maybe our next date should be just him and me," Jessie said carefully.

Ollie felt his insides suddenly explode with cuckold angst. The idea made him burn with jealousy and anger. How dare Roman suggest taking his wife out alone? But at the same time, the idea of Roman and Jessie going out alone, as boyfriend and girlfriend on a date, was so wickedly delicious!

"Do you want to go on a date alone with Roman?" he asked.

Jessie hesitated only a moment. She didn't want to hurt her husband's feelings, but she knew he got off on his angst, and anyway, she wanted to be honest with him. She said, "Yes, I think I'd like that."

"Oh fuck Jessie! You want to be alone with him!" Ollie groaned, and then he was cumming, his cock erupting with a burst of his jizz that coated the fingers around his shaft.

Jessie heard her husband climax. As she listened to Ollie panting from his orgasm, she shook her head in disbelief. She couldn't believe how her life had changed so drastically in just a few months.

But if she was honest with herself, she wouldn't change anything. Because she wanted to see Roman again. Be with him again.

She wanted to feel Roman inside her again. Forcing her again. Making her cum again.

And she wanted to feel Roman bareback in her, and shooting his sperm inside her again.

CHAPTER 6

J essie waited a couple days to call Roman about going on a date. She needed the time to settle herself after the experience in his office.

When she finally called, he teased, "What, are you playing hard to get now?" He was joking, but not really. He'd called and texted many times the last 48 hours. She hadn't responded to any of them.

"I've been busy. You know. With work," Jessie lied.

"Yeah right," Roman said with a sarcastic laugh. He knew she hated her job. She'd mentioned it to him. She wanted to dance for a living, but that dream had fizzled out. She was moderately successful in marketing, but the job didn't inspire her or feed her soul. She definitely worked to live, not the other way around.

"So anyways," Jessie said, wanting to change the subject. "Do you want to go out Saturday? On a date?"

"I thought the guy was supposed to ask the girl," Roman said sarcastically. "Which I would've, if you answered your phone."

"I told you. I was busy," Jessie told him.

"Whatever," Roman said. He was irritated, because Jessie was calling all the shots, and he wasn't used to that power dynamic with chicks. But he put up with it, because she was very pretty and smoking hot. He liked her too. She had a short temper and a lot of spunk, but she only looked prettier when she was angry about something. And her pussy was the best he'd ever felt. Like a warm, tight velvet glove around his cock.

Jessie sensed his irritation. To smooth things over, she said "It'll just be you and me. Ollie won't be there this time."

"How's Metro Ollie feel about that?" he asked.

Jessie frowned. She didn't like when he called her husband that. But she let it go, as she didn't want any more tension in their conversation.

"It was his idea actually," Jessie said. "I mean, about going out on a date. I told him you said it should just be us on our next date."

"And he was okay with that?"

Jessie didn't respond. She didn't want to reveal that Ollie had cum when she told him she did want to go alone on a date with Roman.

Roman laughed at her silence. "Whatever," he said, the laugh still in his voice.

"So are we going out?" Jessie asked.

"Of course we're going out," Roman told her. "We'll go someplace fun. Then we'll go to your place. And Metro Ollie will watch me fuck you. He'll watch me make you cum on my cock."

Jessie felt her cheeks flush. "Can you be nice?" she chastised.

"I'm just joking," Roman said with another laugh. "Don't worry. I won't call him that to his face. I like Ollie. He's a nice guy."

"He *is* a nice guy," Jessie agreed.

"But you have to do something for me," Roman said.

"What?"

"When's he get home?"

"Friday," Jessie answered.

"That's what I figured. Are you going to let him fuck you?"

Jessie's eyes opened wide with shock. "*Yes*," she said crossly.

"I'm not into seconds," Roman told her. "Not into creampies. You know what a creampie is?"

"Yes, I know what a freaking creampie is," Jessie said indignantly. "So what are you getting at?"

"Will you fuck just Friday, or Saturday too before our date?" Roman asked.

"I don't know," Jessie said. "I'll do whatever Ollie wants. I never say no to my husband."

"Even if you're not into it?"

"Who says I'm not into it?"

"Whatever," Roman said with a laugh. "Do you know sperm can be in a girl's pussy for 24 hours?"

"I don't know. I guess so."

"So here's what I want," Roman said. "Twenty four hours before we see each other, he can't cum inside you. He wraps it up."

"Are you *freaking* crazy?" Jessie said immediately. "I can't ask him to do that. He's my husband."

"You've already done it before," Roman said. "I heard you talking to him the time I was over."

"But that was like, right before we had sex," Jessie said. "You're talking about making Ollie wear a condom all Friday. And Saturday morning."

"Are you going to make me wear a condom on Saturday?" Roman asked.

"Oh, so you're asking me this now?" Jessie said sarcastically. She was referring to the other day in his office, when he bent her over his desk and fucked her bareback and came inside her.

"You liked it," Roman said confidently.

Jessie's cheeks flushed. "You're so sure of yourself," she scoffed.

Roman didn't reply immediately. Jessie could practically hear him grinning into the phone.

"I'm just saying, if I've got to wrap it up, Metro Ollie should too," he said. "Fair is fair."

Jessie grimaced. No it wasn't fair. Ollie was her husband. Roman was her ... her *whatever*. Asking Ollie to wear a condom in the heat of the moment was one thing. But making him wear a condom every time they did it on Friday and Saturday – that seemed wrong.

"There's another option," Roman said.

"What?"

"I'll deal with Ollie's creampie, if I get to fuck you bareback too," Roman said. "And you don't ask me to pull out, because I won't."

Jessie's lips parted in surprise. "You know I'm not on birth control," she said. "Are you trying to get me pregnant?"

Roman laughed and joked, "I told you. I can't help thinking that way. It's instinctive. Procreation of species."

"This isn't a joke Roman. The other day, you said you want to put a baby in me, the way Jamal put a tattoo on Alisha," Jessie reminded him.

"Look, you caught me off guard, I was pissed. I already said sorry."

Jessie frowned into the phone. "Roman, just so you know," she said. "If I get pregnant, it's Ollie's baby. You understand that?"

Roman didn't respond. After a few moments, Jessie said again, "Do you understand Roman?"

Roman shrugged and said "Whatever." His noncommittal answer made Jessie's frown deepen.

"So which is it?" he asked. "Condoms for 24 hours, or no condoms?"

Jessie hesitated, then said "I'll let you know."

———— ◉ ————

Ollie got home late Friday. He immediately pulled Jessie onto their bed. She'd dressed special for him, in a tight skirt, stockings and heels. She'd also brushed her hair to a silky luster and spent extra time on her makeup.

"Tell me again about how he bent you over and fucked you from behind," Ollie said excitedly as he kissed and fondled her. He was naked now. Jesse was still completely dressed. She even still had the heels on. Ollie preferred it this way. He liked to take his time undressing his sexy wife. It was always like unwrapping a Christmas gift.

"He was really rough," Jessie said. "He did this to me." She reached back to partially unzip her dress. Then she tugged the dress a bit to the side. Ollie's eyes went wide as he saw the bruise on her shoulder, right next to her bra strap – the hickey.

Ollie's anger flared, and so did his lust.

Jessie said, "I think I'm seeing the real Roman."

Ollie looked questioning at her.

"When we first met him, we thought he was a nice guy. Good husband, good father. Handsome and all, but you know, just a nice man."

"And now?" Ollie asked.

"I think that was his church face," Jessie said. "He's really aggressive and arrogant. And super-alpha."

Ollie looked at her. He said, "You mean like all your old boyfriends."

"Yeah, but, all those guys were boys," Jessie said. "Roman's a man."

Ollie stared at his wife. Her words inflamed his desires, but also bothered him.

"So what am I? A man or a boy?" he asked.

"You're a man, baby," Jessie assured him. Then she reached between their bodies and cupped his thin, 4 inch hard cock. With a playful crooked grin, she teased "Except this part of you."

"Oh god Jessie baby," Ollie groaned as she gently caressed his cock. "You're going out with him tomorrow night?"

"I am," Jessie said. "I asked him."

Ollie shook his head. "He should ask you. I want it to be real."

"He would've but I wasn't answering his calls. I was still getting over what he did to me," Jessie explained. "But what do you mean by real?"

"You're dating, right?" Ollie said with a lustful hoarse voice. He tugged up the skirt of her dress as he kissed her lips and neck. Her silky legs and lace stocking tops came into view. He pushed her shapely legs apart and got between them.

"I want your dating to be real," he said as he cupped both her small breasts with his hands. "And when you're dating, especially in the beginning, the guy asks the girl on dates."

"I want it to be more than sex," Ollie continued as he massaged her tits through her dress and bra. "I want you to have a relationship with him."

"What if I develop feelings for him?" Jessie asked.

"You already have feelings for him," Ollie reminded his wife as he kissed her lips. "You're crushing on him, right? You're infatuated with him. Right?"

Jessie didn't deny it. "This could be dangerous Ollie," she warned. "Roman's different from my old boyfriends. He's older, more mature. He's a father. A good father."

"What does that mean?" Ollie asked.

"It means he's not a complete asshole like my old boyfriends," Jessie said with a half laugh. "There's a tenderness too." With another laugh, she added "When he's not bending me over a desk and fucking me."

"Jessie baby," Ollie moaned as he kissed her again. "It gets me so hot that he fucks you so good. I hate it, but I love it too, that he fucks you better than me. That he makes you cum better than me."

"So don't over think it," Ollie told his wife as he pulled down the front of her dress. He was in major cuck space now, and thinking with his dick instead of his head. Or his heart.

Ollie pulled the bra straps down Jessie's arms, exposing her perfect little A cups. "Let's have fun with our game. Then, in a while, we'll stop fooling around with Roman and start a family."

Ollie pulled Jessie's panties down her stocking legs and wiggled them free of her high heels. Then he positioned himself to enter her.

But Jessie stopped him. She reached over to the bedside cabinet for a condom and handed it to him. "Will you put this on?" she asked him.

Ollie looked at her, not understanding.

"Roman said he doesn't like creampies," Jessie told him. "It's his 24 hour rule. He wants you to wear a condom the 24 hours before I'm with him."

"Roman has rules? For me?" Ollie said looking incredulous.

"Or he said you don't have to wear a condom, as long as he doesn't have to either," Jessie said.

Ollie's eyes went wide. Then he frowned and grumbled, "So he's controlling things now?"

"No. I'm just telling you what he said," Jessie said. "Anyways, there's no way I'm letting him inside me without a condom. It's the worse time of the month for me. I know I'm ovulating."

"Then shouldn't I cum inside you? To start a family?"

"Aren't we waiting to do that? You just said that," Jessie said gently. "You said we'll play our game for a while, and then later start a family."

"Is that what you want?" Ollie asked.

Jessie shrugged, then said, "I think I do. Please don't hate me Ollie, but I *am* crushing on Roman. I love you, I do, but being in a new relationship, you know, with all that NRE, it's so exciting. I guess I want to experience that one more time before really settling down."

Ollie's heart was pounding and his insides were twisted into a tight knot. He found it hard to breathe. Practically gasping, he managed to say, "I'm glad you're honest with me. It helps."

"I think playing this game, we have to be honest with each other," Jessie said.

"We do," Ollie agreed.

Making the decision for both of them, Jessie took the condom back from Ollie. She tore the foil package with her teeth.

"You could just lie and tell Roman I wore a condom," Ollie said as he looked at the flat round latex in her hand.

Jessie shook her head as she rolled the rubber down her husband's hard shaft. "I won't lie to him," she said. "He's supposed to be my boyfriend, right?"

Ollie's jealousy flared at Jessie's words, but his hard cock jerked with delicious cuckold angst.

Jessie reached down and guided Ollie's now-sheathed cock into her
pussy. He moaned as he entered her. Even with the condom on, her
pussy still felt *so good*.

"You should tell him he has to stop seeing other girls," Ollie said.

Jessie stared down at her husband as she slowly move up and down
on his cock. "He'd want to see me more," Jessie said. "He's got a lot
of fuck buddies. I think he's making up for all those years of being
married."

"All those years of being married to Alisha, with just her pussy. I'm
sure he likes your pussy better."

"He said that," she said. "He said my pussy feels better than hers. It's
tighter."

"Your pussy is pristine," Ollie said. "It's not ruined like Alisha's."

"Ruined?" Jessie said with a laugh. She was still slowly moving up
and down on his cock. "How's her pussy ruined?"

"Her pussy's been fucked by Roman's big cock for years," Ollie said.
"And she's given birth 3 times. So of course her pussy is loose and
doesn't feel as good as yours."

Jessie laughed at her husband's crazy thoughts. She knew he got this
way when he was lustful. When he had his fuck face on, like now.

"And Roman said he wants to get you pregnant," Ollie reminded
her.

"He didn't say that exactly," Jessie said. "But you know what he said,
when he talked about the no condom option?"

"What?"

"He said if you pick no condoms, then he won't pull out," Jessie
said. "He'll cum inside me. I said, *You know I'm not on the pill. Do you
want to get me pregnant?*"

Ollie stared at his wife. "Then what happened?"

"I told him, if I *do* get pregnant, it's your baby, no matter what,"
Jessie said.

"What did he say?"

"He didn't look happy," Jessie said. "I don't think he likes it when he's not controlling things."

Ollie's head was spinning. All this was so much to process all of a sudden.

"Are you going to tell him to stop seeing other girls?" he asked. His breathing was heavy from excitement. "He shouldn't hook up with other girls if you're his girlfriend. You should be exclusive to each other."

"He'd want to see me more," Jessie said. "Would you be okay with that?"

"Do you want to see him more?"

Jessie looked thoughtful and said "I think maybe I would."

Then the married couple was silent as Jessie rode Ollie's cock. It wasn't much longer before he came.

CHAPTER 7

The logistics of Jessie rendezvousing with Roman for their date was an issue.

Jessie wanted to meet Roman some place, as she didn't want to risk people they knew seeing him pick her up at their apartment. She was still worried about the rumors flying around church and she didn't want more rumors where they lived.

But Ollie wanted things to feel real, so he wanted Roman picking Jessie up from their apartment. In the end, Ollie wore Jessie down and she reluctantly agreed to let Roman pick her up.

Ollie also worked out a story she would tell if seen with Roman. Jessie would say that Roman was an old friend and it was his birthday. Ollie and Jessie were taking Roman for dinner and drinks to celebrate, but then Ollie had to go on a last minute business trip, so Jessie was taking Roman out alone as they didn't want to disappoint him. Ollie said this story was good since it had elements of the truth.

But Jessie wasn't so sure. The fact was, in reality (instead of the bizarro life they were living now), if Ollie had to go away, then she wouldn't go out alone with Roman no matter how old a friend he was. After all, Jessie was worldly enough to know if a girl and a guy go out alone, and there's alcohol involved, then anything could happen. In real life, she wouldn't put herself in that kind of position where she might end up being unfaithful to Ollie.

Jessie knew Ollie's story would raise eyebrows for sure. It had too many holes, people would suspect something was up.

But she suspected Ollie *wanted* people to suspect she was having an affair with Roman. Just like there were rumors at church. It turned him on if people suspected she was fucking other men behind his back.

Jessie wasn't crazy about the idea of people they knew thinking she was an adulteress. But she loved Ollie and she knew fair was fair. She got the physical pleasure of a sexual relationship with Roman, a very handsome and hunky man. And she was able to enjoy the excitement and infatuation of a new relationship.

What did Ollie get? He didn't get the physical or emotional pleasure of a new girl. Instead, he got the mindfuck of his wife with a new man. And if that mindfuck included wanting people to suspect she was cheating on him, then Jessie figured that was only fair.

As long as they were careful, and no one found out *for real* she was fucking Roman, then she figured it would all be okay in the end. Once she was barefoot and pregnant with Ollie's baby, all those rumors of her infidelity would go away.

———————◉———————

They agreed that Roman would pick up Jessie after sunset when it was dark. That way, their neighbors would be less likely to recognize her with him.

When Roman got to their apartment, they initially treated him like a platonic friend. He was holding a bottle and a black plastic bag.

"This is for you buddy," Roman said to Ollie as he handed him the bottle. "I think I heard you say it's your favorite."

Ollie looked at the label of the bottle and his eyes went wide. It was Highland Park scotch, the 30 year release. Ollie knew this release of Highland Park was close to $1000. He'd never tasted it because it was way outside his wallet.

"Thank you," Ollie said, feeling grateful.

Jessie smiled a *thank you* into Roman's eyes, and then took the bottle from Ollie. "I'll get you a glass," she told her husband.

As she moved to the kitchen, Roman said "I'll give you a hand." He followed her into the kitchen.

"I don't need help pouring a glass of scotch," Jessie said with a laugh.

"I just want to look at you," Roman said. He took the scotch from her and put it on the counter. Then, with his hands on her upper arms, he turned her to look at him.

Roman looked Jessie up and down. He liked what she saw.

Jessie looked like a movie star, with her beautiful face and long, lush blonde hair. She wore a body hugging dress that ended a few inches above her knees, black hose and shiny black high heels.

Jessie could tell he liked how she looked, and his approval made her heart do flips.

"Will you do something for me?" Roman asked.

"What?"

"Take off your bra," Roman said. "I remember those times, you know, before we got together, when I'd see you braless. So I'd like to see you that way tonight."

Jessie grinned and gave him a playful roll of her eyes. But she didn't mind going braless. A benefit of having small breasts was she didn't need the support of a bra. And if Roman saw her nipples through the thin material of her dress, well, why did it matter? The whole point of tonight was for him to fuck her. So if going braless got him hot, then she'd go braless.

"Should I take off my bra here?" Jessie asked with a wave at the kitchen they were in.

"No," Roman said. "Give Ollie his scotch. Then go into the bathroom and take off your bra. Give Ollie the bra when you come out. It'll probably get him hot if he knows you're braless. Especially if he knows I told you to take it off. Right?"

"Probably," Jessie agreed with a laugh. Grinning at him, she put an ice cube into a tumbler and poured a finger of the Highland Park. Then, still grinning at Roman, she left the kitchen and walked back to her husband.

Ollie was sitting in the sofa. Jessie leaned over. As she handed the tumbler of Highland Park to him, she whispered into his ear, "He wants me to take off my bra."

With a grin at her husband, Jessie walked towards the bathroom. Ollie had a lump in his throat as he watched her go.

Roman came out of the kitchen and sat on the sofa next to him. They watched the Mets on the TV without saying anything.

Jessie emerged from the bathroom a moment later. She dropped the bra into Ollie's lap. Then she stood and faced Roman. "Is this what you want?" she asked with a laugh.

Both Roman and Ollie looked at Jessie's chest. Without the bra, her nipples could be seen, making bumps in the thin material of her dress. "Perfect," Roman said with a grin as he stood up.

"Can you hold these for me?" she asked Roman. She handed her ID, keys and lipstick to him. She didn't like carrying a purse when anything alcohol was involved, because she was notorious for losing things.

Normally, of course, Jessie would ask Ollie to hold these things for her. He'd been doing it for years, since they first started dating.

Now she was asking Roman. He felt jealousy and angst cut into his gut.

Jessie leaned over and kissed Ollie. "We'll be back soon," she said. "I love you."

"I love you too," Ollie said.

Then Jessie and Roman were off on their date. Ollie was left holding her bra and feeling, once again, that he was making a horrible mistake to share his wife with Roman.

———⊙———

Roman and Jessie walked a couple feet apart, like platonic friends, just in case they ran into someone Jessie knew. Fortunately, they managed to make it out of the apartment building and into the taxi

without being noticed. Inside the taxi, Roman reached for Jessie's hand.
She let him hold her hand.

"What's in the bag?" Jessie asked, looking at the black plastic bag
still in Roman's hand.

"It's a surprise," Roman said with a grin. Jessie smiled, wondering
what it was.

"Where are we going?" she asked.

"Have you ever seen *Hamilton*?" Roman asked.

Jessie stared at him. "Are you serious?" she asked incredulously.

Roman grinned at her. Referring to Ollie's cover story, he joked "It's
my birthday, right? So I wanna do something fun." Jessie grinned. She
was super excited to see *Hamilton*.

Roman leaned over and kissed Jessie. She kissed him back, and
opened her lips to welcome his tongue. They kissed for long moments,
and when they finally pulled away, they were both breathing hard.

Roman wrapped his arm around Jessie's shoulders and she melted
into him. She saw the taxi driver watching them in the rear-view mirror.

Roman kissed Jessie again. Their tongues danced in their mouths.
They were so hot for each other. Roman reached between their bodies
and put his hand over one of Jessie's braless breasts. She was
uncomfortable as she knew the taxi driver was watching, but then he
thumbed her hard nipple through the silky fabric of the dress, and she
moaned into his mouth.

With his other hand, he took Jessie's hand and put it on his crotch.
He felt rock hard. Jessie teasingly traced the outline of his cock and
he groaned. Roman moved his hand down to Jessie's legs. She knew
he was about to finger her. She remembered the driver and again felt
uncomfortable. She put both of her hands on his wrist, stopping him
from moving under her dress. She said "Roman baby, stop, we have all
night."

Roman reluctantly moved his hand away from Jessie's legs. Jessie
glanced at the rear-view mirror. The taxi driver was looking at her. He

was older with a dark complexion, maybe Muslin. He had a rigid look
to him, like he'd lived a hard life. For a moment, Jessie imagined the
man getting into the back seat and fucking her, and forcing her to cum.
She shivered at the thought.

They eventually arrived at *Bond 45*, a popular restaurant for theater
goers. As Jessie slid out of the taxi, her skirt rode up and she flashed her
lacy stocking tops. As she pulled her dress down, she glanced at the taxi
driver. He was looking at her and clearly had seen her exposed thighs.

The taxi driver reached out of the cab and handed Jessie his card.
"Call me when you want to go home," he said in a heavy middle eastern
accent. Jessie looked at the card. It said *Amir's Taxi Service*. Jessie gave
the card to Roman. They walked into Bond 45. Just before the door
closed, Jessie glanced back. The taxi driver was still there, looking at her.

They ordered drinks and Jessie gulped down half her dirty martini
as soon as it arrived.

"Still getting over Amir?" Roman asked.

Jessie looked embarrassed. "You saw him looking at me?" she asked.

"I'm sure dudes look at you all the time," Roman said with a laugh.
He waved Amir's card and said "We could skip *Hamilton* and call
Amir. Ever have a threeway?"

Jessie frowned at him and said, "I thought you didn't like
creampies."

"I'd do you first," Roman said with another laugh. He teased, "Then
I'd hold you down while he fucks you."

"Oh my god," Jessie said with a roll of her eyes. She tried to hide her
excitement at what he just said.

"So ... did you do that with Alisha? Threeways?"

"Early on, yeah," Roman said. "An extra guy sometimes, an extra girl
sometimes." With a grin he added, "I liked it better when it was an extra
girl."

"Wow ... I just can't imagine Alisha doing that," Jessie said with
wonder.

"She was wild back then," Roman said. "And super-hot. Big boobs and long legs. Not as pretty as you though. Or as hot."

"And when it was another man," Jessie said hesitantly. "You held her down while he, you know, did her?"

Roman grinned. "You get off on that right?" he said knowingly.

Jessie blushed with embarrassment, which was the same as saying yes. And Roman knew it.

"I had you pegged as a submissive little slut," he said.

"Oh my god, just shut up," Jessie said with an embarrassed laugh.

Roman laughed too. Then said, "No, she's not into that. She likes to be in control. Probably a big surprise, right?" He laughed. Jessie laughed too, although she wasn't sure why.

"I'm not surprised she's with a black dude," Roman continued. "She was always into that. Did you know she's from the south? Mississippi. She was always into the taboo of opening her legs for black cock."

"And you were okay with that?"

"You mean threesomes with other dudes?" Roman said. "Sure. As long as I got to fuck other chicks. And it was a competition. Alisha always told me I fucked her the best. And you know her, not matter what else, she always told you the way it was. If some black guy fucked her better, she'd tell me."

"So you feel like you're competing with Ollie?" Jessie asked.

Roman laughed. "Sure, I'm competing with Metro Ollie," he said dismissively.

Jessie laughed too. She knew she should defend her husband, and not laugh at Roman's joke, but she'd already told Ollie that Roman was her best lover ever. So she didn't feel like she was betraying Ollie by laughing. At least not too much. She still felt a little churn in her stomach though.

"But whatever. Life goes on," Roman said, suddenly getting melancholy about his impending divorce. "If she thinks – what's his name, Jamal? If she thinks Jamal fucks her better, then whatever. I don't care about Alisha anymore. At least I got the best years of her."

"What do you mean?" Jessie asked.

"When she was super-hot," Roman answered. "Don't get me wrong, Alisha's still got a good body. But not like then, before we started having kids. Back then, her body was smoking. Jamal's getting my leftovers. So fuck him. He can have her."

Jessie looked down, remembering how Ollie said Roman had ruined Alisha, and he wanted to ruin her too. Ruin her tight pussy with his big cock. A dominate man doing what he wanted with her body. The thought made Jessie shiver inside. She shifted her legs, knowing her panties were wet.

Roman sensed her mood change, and said "Sorry. That's probably an asshole thing to say."

"No, it's okay," Jessie said, not wanting Roman to feel bad. "It must be hard and, I guess, confusing, when your marriage ends after so many years."

Roman reached over and squeezed her hand. With a grin he said, "You're not a bad rebound chick."

Jessie smiled back, but then remembered where she was. Alone with a man who was not her husband. In a popular Broadway bar that people she knew went to all the time.

Jessie eased her hand away and whispered, "We have to be careful, Roman." She nervously looked around the bar. She was relieved when she didn't see anyone she knew.

Then she forced thoughts of Amir and threeways out of her head. She wanted to focus on *Hamilton*.

Jessie loved Broadway, and going to *Hamilton* was a dream. She knew you could buy tickets nowadays – they weren't impossible to get like before—but they were still very expensive, and she and Ollie couldn't afford it.

"*Hamilton* would be the perfect gig for me," Jessie said. "Dancing, but not too much dancing. I think I could do it."

"Why don't you try out?" Roman asked.

"Oh my god, I'd never get an audition for a show like *Hamilton,*" Jessie said with a laugh. "You have to really know people, even for minor parts. I used to have an agent, but he won't even answer my calls anymore. I won't have sex with producers and directors, or him, so he's not interested in me anymore."

"Are you serious? Casting couches are real?" Roman asked looking shocked.

"Well, I mean, if you're really talented, probably not," Jessie said. "I'm not actually a good dancer. I'm okay, but .... And I can't sing. I mean, I'm okay at karaoke ...," Jessie joked with a laugh, then her voice trailed off.

It was Jessie's turn to feel melancholy. She said, "It was a stupid dream, wanting to make Broadway ... anyways, my job isn't that bad."

"You hate your job," Roman said.

Jessie shrugged and said, "Everyone hates their job, right?" She took another gulp of her dirty martini, finishing it. Roman ordered another round.

"Anyways, I feel bad you spent so much on these tickets," she said.

Roman grinned. He said, "I got them for free. My roommate back in the NFL. He got cut after one season like me, but he was a quarterback and you know how much quarterbacks make, even washouts. He put his money into entertainment. Movies, theater, I'm not exactly sure what. But I called him and he had tickets, so here we are."

"Oh my god, that's so awesome," Jessie gushed appreciatively.

"What team did you play for anyways?" she asked.

"You didn't Google me?" Roman joked.

"I should have," Jessie admitted with a laugh.

Grinning, Roman said "The Jets."

"Oh. Here in New York."

"Yeah. Duh. That's why I opened my gym here."

They both laughed.

"Sometimes people still ask for my autograph," Roman said. "Can you believe I'm on a football card?"

Grinning, Jessie said "Maybe I'll get your autograph someday."

"Sure. Just tell me what part of your body, and I'll be happy to sign."

"I don't think Ollie would like that," Jessie said, and they laughed again.

Smiling into his eyes, she said, "Anyways, I really appreciate all the trouble you went to, to get the tickets."

Grinning, Roman said "I wanted to make our first date special." His voice had a smile in it, since of course this was only a pretend date. A married woman can't go on a *real* date with another man.

"This is our second date," she corrected him, that same joking smile in her voice.

"I mean, our first date without Metro Ollie," he said with a laugh. Jessie laughed too.

Jessie took his hand and, under the table, she put it on her knee. "I'll pay you back later," she said with a mischievous grin.

"I was hoping you'd go down on me in the taxi," Roman teased.

Jessie laughed. "You wish," she teased back, her blue eyes sparkling. "And maybe Amir wished he saw that." Roman laughed.

Then she said, "And later, just in case you get too—."

Jessie paused, trying to think of the right word. She finally said, "*Enthusiastic*. Like last time ...."

They laughed.

"Ollie picked condoms," Jessie said, completing her sentence. "Your options. Condoms or no condoms. Ollie picked condoms."

"My loss," Roman said with a shrug. Then looking into Jessie's eyes, he added "I think your loss too. Right? You like how it feels, when I cum in you."

Roman's words made Jessie shiver. She shifted her legs again, knowing her panties were probably soaking now.

Roman grinned. "You're not the only chick who gets off on that," he said knowingly.

Jessie's cheeks went red with embarrassment. Again!

"Will you shut up?" she said with a helpless laugh. Roman laughed back.

They walked from Bond 45 to the Richard Rogers theater. Jessie felt a little shaky in her high heels after their conversation, and what had happened in the taxi.

They didn't hold hands, but Jessie walked closer to Roman this time. It wasn't like she forgot about Ollie. But at that moment, she *did* feel like she was on a date with Roman. She felt closer to him.

And Ollie felt distant from her. Jessie knew it was NRE, it was just the infatuation that was always there in any new relationship. She forced herself not to feel guilty about it – not to feel like she was betraying Ollie – since she knew this is what her husband wanted her to do.

Roman's friend had really come through. Their seats were just off center and only 8 rows back.

Jessie was enthralled by the performance. She'd seen the movie and listened to the music of course, but the musical was so much more amazing and powerful in person. Jessie felt so grateful to Roman for allowing her to experience this wonderful musical.

Intermission was 20 minutes. As the people around them got up for a stretch and bathroom break, Roman turned to Jessie. "Do you like this?" he asked.

"It's so freaking amazing," Jessie gushed enthusiastically.

Roman put his hand on Jessie's knee. "I think *you're* amazing," he said. "Sorry if I was a jerk before talking about Alisha. I can't help it though. You're way prettier than her. And hotter. Then and now."

"You shouldn't compare me to her. It's disrespectful," Jessie said softly, looking down demurely. "You're getting a divorce, but you were together a long time, and have 3 wonderful children."

"Okay – then I'll compare you to Fletcher. And Bianca. And all the other girls. You're the hottest of them all."

"All the other girls ...," Jessie said, pushing Roman's hand off her knee. She was suddenly irritated hearing about all his conquests. Especially since she had been feeling so close to him just a moment ago. It was a slap in her face.

"You talk about your other fuck buddies all the time. Is that supposed to impressed me?"

"What do you mean?"

"I just don't like feeling like one of your many conquests," Jessie said.

"You're not. I just said you're amazing," Roman said. "I don't think of you as just a fuck buddy. We're friends too, right?"

Jessie hesitated, wondering if she was really going to say this. Finally, she said, "Ollie thinks you should only see me. Only have sex with me. He thinks you should stop seeing other girls."

Roman stared at her. "I assume you're not planning to split with Ollie," he said.

"Of course not."

"Then what the fuck are you talking about?" he asked.

"Look ... it's up to you," Jessie said. "We can just hook up sometimes. Or we can have a relationship. I mean, I'll admit I'm crushing on you. Maybe you're crushing on me, I don't know. But if we are, you know, into each other – then I don't think you should see other girls. While we're dating."

"But you've still with Ollie," Roman said with a frown. "You're still having sex with him."

Jessie held up her hands in an *I can't help the way it is* gesture, and said "I know this is all crazy. I'm married. Happily married. But I'm with you too. I'm just telling you the way I feel."

There was a ding-dong, and the lights blinked twice. Intermission was ending.

Jessie and Roman settled back into their seats to watch the second act. There was a chill between them.

As Thomas Jefferson's introductory *What'd I Miss?* scene ended, Roman leaned over and whispered into Jessie's ear, "Are you really crushing on me?"

Jessie nodded yes.

Roman whispered, "I'm crushing on your too."

They stared into each other's eyes for long moments. Jessie wanted Roman to kiss her, but she knew that wasn't possible, not here in public.

Roman reached his hand over though, and in the darkness of the theater, Jessie let him hold her hand in her lap.

Jessie tried to focus on the show, but her thoughts and emotions were swirling. She felt she and Roman had just taken a major step in their relationship, but how could they have a relationship at all? She was married after all.

Yet, she had feelings for Roman. Romantic feelings. She felt like she was betraying Ollie, but he wanted her to feel this way. Sex with Roman was bad enough. Ollie wanted her to go further. He *wanted* her to date Roman. He *wanted* her to be infatuated with him. He *wanted* Roman to only see her, and no other girls. He *wanted* them to develop feelings for each other.

The show ended. Despite all the distractions, Jessie thoroughly enjoyed it. As the lights came on, she pulled her hand away from his.

They stayed in their seats for a few minutes as the crowd filtered out of the theater. Roman leaned over and whispered, "If I'm going to stop seeing other girls, I'm gonna want to see you more."

"I get that," Jessie whispered.

"When you're with me, you're with me," Roman told her. "Even if Ollie is there. When we're together, you're with me, not him."

"Okay," Jessie agreed in a low, soft voice.

"And I want you to sleep over sometimes," Roman said. "On nights Alisha has the kids."

"I have to ask Ollie," Jessie said hesitantly. "He doesn't want me to do that."

Roman frowned at her. "It can't always be what Ollie wants," he said. "If I'm gonna stop seeing other girls, then I get some say over you."

Jessie shivered inside, at the thought of Roman having power over her. Over her body.

"I get that," she said softly. "I just have to talk to Ollie. Okay?"

They stared at each other for long moments. Finally, Roman nodded his agreement. With the crowd thinning, they got up and walked to the exit.

Jessie expected Roman to take her home, but instead he told the cab driver to go to the High Line.

"Have you ever been to the High Line?" he asked her. The High Line was a public park on the West Side of Manhattan. It was built on a historic, elevated rail line. It had gardens, art exhibits and restaurants.

"Yes, we love it. Ollie and I go there all the time," Jessie said.

"I want to show you something there," Roman told her.

"Is that the surprise?" Jessie asked, looking at the black plastic bag still in Roman's hand.

"Maybe," Roman said mysteriously, and they both laughed.

A few minutes later, they arrived at the High Line 23. It was a high end apartment complex where each apartment took up an entire floor. It was called HL23 by residents. When units came on the market – and they rarely did – they sold for millions of dollars.

HL23 apartments were famous for floor-to-ceiling windows that looked directly down onto the High Line park. People walking on the

High Line could see directly into the apartments if the curtains weren't closed.

"My quarterback friend has a place here," Roman said. "He's in Europe or something. Come on, let's check it out."

They rode the elevator to the 6th floor unit. The elevator opened up into unit number 6. Unit #6, like all the HL23 apartments, took up the entire floor.

What was immediately noticeable – and striking – was the floor to ceiling windows. They were huge, taking up three sides of the apartment. The windows had cinematic views of the High Line park, Hudson Yards and the Manhattan skyline.

Jessie walked over, with Roman close behind. It was late but the High Line was still crowded with lots of people mingling and going to restaurants and bars, watching the street entertainment, getting snacks from the many pop up vendors, and just people watching.

Jessie could clearly see the people on the High Line through the crystal-clear floor-to-ceiling windows. And even though they were a few stories up, it felt like all those people were in the apartment with them.

Jessie also knew the people could see them in the apartment. A few times, she and Ollie watched parties going on in these HL23 apartments. And Roman had turned on a couple of lamps behind them, making it even easier to see into the apartment.

"So what are we doing here?" Jessie asked, but deep down she already knew.

"I'm gonna fuck you," Roman said. He pointed and said, "Against that window."

Roman was pointing at the window that looked directly over the High Line. All the people down there would be able to see them.

"No way Roman," Jessie said warily. "You promised you'd be careful."

"I am being careful," Roman said. And he handed the black plastic bag to her.

Jessie looked in the bag. She took out what was inside.

It was a wig. A wig with short black hair.

"Are you freaking serious?" Jessie asked as she stared at the wig in her hand.

Roman grinned at her. "It's a disguise," he said. "No one will recognize you. So put it on."

"Why don't we do it in the bedroom?" Jessie said motioning to the next room. The bedroom had big windows too but they didn't open up to the High Line.

"If I'm gonna stop seeing other girls then I get some control," Roman told her. "It's not you calling all the shots."

Jessie pursed her lips at Roman. She always did that when she didn't like something. But after a moment, she relented and went into the bathroom to put on the wig.

Jessie's natural blonde hair was long – *bra-strap length*, as Ollie liked to say – it was thick and lush and had a natural wave to it. When she brushed it out, as she had tonight for her date with Roman, it had a luxurious sheen that shined in the light.

Ollie loved her blonde hair. It was the first thing that attracted him to her. He had a strong preference for blondes, and had never dated any girl who wasn't blonde.

When they first met in college, Jessie's hair was shoulder length, because long hair was a pain to take care of. It took a lot of effort to wash, dry and style long hair, especially since her hair was so full. Once they became exclusive and committed, Jessie began growing her hair longer as Ollie asked her to. Now it was even with the middle of her back. Ollie often said he wanted her hair *"bra strap length."*

Jessie had worn wigs before – in school plays and Halloween parties – so she knew how to put on a wig despite her long, thick hair.

She saw immediately the wig was high quality and most likely made from real hair.

After putting on the wig, Jessie looked at herself in the mirror. She almost didn't recognize herself. Her hair was black and a few inches short of her shoulders.

She left the bathroom and returned to Roman. He stared at her. While Ollie had a thing for long haired blondes, Roman liked girls with short dark hair.

"Do I look like your old girlfriends now? All those girls in your pictures?" Jessie asked.

"Jessie, you look amazing!" Roman enthused as he continued to stared at her face, now framed by short dark hair.

He moved to her and put his hand behind her neck. It was easy now since her hair was short.

"*Absolutely – fucking – amazing*," Roman repeated, as he lowered his head and kissed her.

Jessie kissed him back. She parted her lips and Roman caressed her tongue with his. He pulled off his jacket and shirt. Jessie ran her fingers over his muscular chest. Her body tingled, her passion growing. She loved Roman's muscular chest, she loved the feel of his well defined pecs and abs, and the dark hair running up his chest.

Roman moved her to the big floor-to-ceiling window that looked out to the High Line and all the people there. Her back was against the window, so the people outside could only see her sexy tight ass and long stockinged legs.

Roman stopped kissing Jessie, moving back a step. He reached into his pocket for her lipstick, and handed it to her. "Fix your lipstick," he ordered her.

Jessie did. Her lips were once again shiny red. "You're so beautiful," Roman said, looking at her face and her red, wet lips. "And so fucking hot."

"You want me to stop seeing other girls?" Roman asked.

"Yes."

"Then who do you belong to?"

"I belong to you," Jessie said.

"Are you my little submissive slut?"

With her beautiful blue eyes downcast, Jessie softly replied, "Yes."

"Turn around," Roman ordered. "Let the people down there see you."

Hesitantly, Jessie turned around so she was facing the window. Her face, camouflaged only by the short black wig, was clearly visible to the crowd of people on the High Line. Some of them were already looking up at her. Many more would be joining them.

Roman pressed his body against hers. His front to her back. He lowered his head and kissed her neck. It was easy now that she had short hair.

Jessie moaned as Roman kissed up her neck to just behind her ear. It was one of her most sensitive erogenous spots, and she moaned. She saw more people looking up at her.

Roman unzipped Jessie's dress and pulled it down so it was around her waist. But her arms were still in the sleeves so she couldn't move them. Since she was braless, her little perfect A cup breasts were now exposed to all the people on the High Line. Now everyone was looking up at her. Hundreds of people. Parents were ushering their children away.

Roman continued to kiss Jessie neck as he reached around her and cupped her naked breasts. He fondled her tits and thumbed her nipples, touching her the way he knew she liked to be touched. Jessie was moaning and her knees felt weak.

Jessie kept her eyes closed, not wanting to see the people below. But she opened her eyes a moment and looked at the crowd. So many people were looking up at her. And many people had their phones out. They were taking pictures of her! They were videoing her!

"Roman they're taking pictures!" she said with alarm.

"I know," Roman growled with lust. "Do you want me to take off the wig?"

"Oh god no! Please no!" Jessie begged.

Roman jerked up her skirt, so now her entire dress was gathered like a belt around her waist. She still couldn't move her arms. She felt completely helpless and vulnerable.

And exposed. Jessie knew the people below on the High Line could see her naked breasts, and all of her long shapely legs in the black thigh high stockings.

Jessie heard Roman taking out his cock. "Roman please," she begged. "Condom. Please."

Jessie knew she was ovulating. And she new Roman came a lot, and he'd fathered 3 children. If he unleashed his virile sperm into her unprotected fertile pussy, he'd almost assuredly impregnate her.

Jessie remembered what Ollie said, and wondered if that was what Roman wanted. *To breed her.* To ruin her young tight body the way he had Alisha's.

Then she heard Roman rip open a condom package. She sensed him rolling the latex down his long, thick shaft.

Then Roman ripped off her thong panties, making Jessie yelp. With one hand, he raised Jessie's right leg, opening her up to him. He knelt since he was taller than Jessie. With his other hand, he guided his cock to her pussy. He rubbed up and down her slit, lubricating his sheathed cock, then pushed into her, penetrating her womanhood with his big cock.

"Oh god!" Jessie gasped at the sudden penetration. As always, being so full and so stretched hurt at first, but then the pain turned to pleasure.

Roman rammed Jessie hard from behind. Since he was taller and his cock so long, each thrust lifted her pretty feet out of her shiny black, *So Kate* high heels.

Jessie risked opening her eyes. It was a raucous party now on the High Line, with her the entertainment. People were laughing and pointing up at her as she got fucked like a cheap slut.

It was all too much for Jessie. So exposed and getting fucked with all those people watching. Feeling enslaved and humiliated with her arms pinned in the sleeves of her dress. Roman's long thick cock rubbing against her clit and stimulating every pleasure nerve in her pussy. Within moments, Jessie came. She screamed as intense orgasmic pleasure exploded in her body.

Jessie's climax was obvious to the large crowd looking up at her. They laughed and clapped. *They applauded her orgasm.*

Jessie could hear their claps and laughter. She could see them pointing up at her. Making fun of her. Laughing at her.

She'd never felt so humiliated in her life. *God – it was such a turn on!*

Roman was still fucking her. Hard and fast. With a hard voice, he hissed "Are you my little submissive slut?"

"Yeah, yeah ...," Jessie chanted as he relentlessly pounded her pussy.

"You're my slut!" Roman growled. "Not Ollie's! Say it!"

"I'm your slut!" Jessie said.

"Not Ollie's! Say it!" Roman demanded.

"I'm your little submissive slut!" Jessie said. "Not Ollie's! Yours!"

Roman abruptly pulled his cock from Jessie's pussy. He forced her down onto her knees. At the same time, he ripped off the condom.

He roughly held Jessie's head while he rapidly jerked himself off, his cock pointed at her face. Within moments he orgasmed, and thick ropes of his milky cum splashed against Jessie's pretty face.

After he was done, breathing hard, he forced Jessie to turn her head, to look out the window, so all the people on the High Line could see her cum splattered face.

CHAPTER 8

Jessie and Roman were quiet in the cab.

After their sex, Jessie rushed to the bathroom to clean up. And to get away from the rowdy crowd down on the High Line.

She cleaned her pretty face of Roman's cum, and fixed her makeup. She pulled up and zipped her dress. After she was done, she mostly looked as she had when they arrived at unit 6 of HL23.

Only her stockings showed evidence of what they'd done. They were laddered at her knees, where Roman had been rough when he came on her face. And her face was flushed, she was breathing hard, and her heart was pounding. And she was scared.

The wig was back in the black plastic bag. There were cum stains on it.

Roman reached over for Jessie's hand. She tried pulling away, but he was insistent, not letting her hand go. "You had the wig on Jessie," he told her.

"They saw my face," Jessie said, panic and fear in her voice. "They took pictures. Videos."

"No one will recognize you with the wig on," Roman assured her.

"Why did you do that?" Jessie asked.

Roman leaned over and whispered in her ear, "Because I know that's how you wanna be treated. That's how you wanna be fucked."

Jessie stared at Roman. She didn't reply, but she didn't deny it. And she no longer tried to pull her hand away.

Roman turned her hand so it was palm up. He touched her wrist with a fingertip, and said "Do you know there's 8 bones in your wrist?"

"Thanks for the anatomy lesson," Jessie said sarcastically. Roman grinned.

"It's very sensitive," he said, running his fingertip in a circle over her wrist.

"Stop," Jessie whined. She tried to pull her hand away but Roman held tight.

"If you touch too hard or too soft, it tickles," Roman said as he traced circles on Jessie's wrist. "But if you caress just the right way, it can be very erotic."

Jessie was breathing hard now, and her cheeks were flushed. The way Roman was caressing her wrist was arousing her.

"Why are you doing this?" she asked between heavy breaths.

"I want to get you horny again," Roman said with a grin. He was speaking low so the taxi driver couldn't hear. "We've got to give Metro Ollie a show, right? So he can rub one out? Jerk off his little dick?"

"Don't say it that way," Jessie said. "It's disrespectful."

"How is it disrespectful?" Roman asked. "He's gonna watch me fuck you, right? And he'll jerk off. And he's got a small dick. So how is it disrespectful? It's not even fake news."

Jessie scowled at him. "Maybe I'll make you go home," she warned.

"You won't do that," Roman said confidently.

"Don't be so sure."

Roman leaned closer and hissed into her ear, "You want me to stop seeing other girls, right? That tells me you want my cock all to yourself. Stop playing hard to get, Jessie. Just remember – I know you're a little submissive slut."

Jessie glared at Roman. But she didn't deny it.

She said "At least stop calling him Metro Ollie. I don't like that."

"I'll make you a deal," Roman said. "I'll stop calling him Metro Ollie. If you call me Romes."

Jessie looked at Roman, not understanding.

"My mom used to call me Romes," he explained. With a sheepish grin, he added "When I was being a good kid. Which, I admit, wasn't

very often. So I'd like it if you called me Romes. You called me that
once, and I liked it."

Jessie couldn't help smiling. *How can he be such an arrogant ass one
second, and then so sweet and vulnerable the next?*, she asked herself as
she felt her heart melting for him.

The taxi arrived at the apartment. As they walked, they didn't hold
hands, but their bodies were closer together than before, almost
touching.

Jessie's head – and her heart – and her pussy – *all of her* were
swirling. She was still processing what had happened at the High Line.
Roman had made her fantasy come true again. He'd humiliated her,
made her feel weak and helpless, and forced her to like it, *forced her to
cum.*

And there was everything else. They talked about so much. She felt
like she was crushing even harder on him. It scared her though, because
she had never been so infatuated with a man, not even Ollie during any
of their time together.

Roman had done terrible things to her, and exposed her to the
world with only that freaking stupid wig to hide her identity. If people
recognized her, knew it was her face covered with cum, it would ruin
her life. Her parents would probably disown her.

And yet, she knew in her heart she would let Roman do it to her
again. She would let him debase her, do terrible humiliating things to
her. And that scared her. Because she didn't know what the limits were.
If there were *even any limits at all* when it came to Roman.

———— ◉ ————

O nce in the apartment, Jessie immediately went to Ollie in the
loveseat. He didn't look good. He had angst all over his face. But
he had his fuck face on too.

"Are you okay?" Jessie asked her husband.

Ollie nodded. "How was it?" he asked. His voice was throaty, lustful.

"Sort of intense," Jessie answered.

When Ollie gave her an inquiring look, she whispered "I'll tell you later."

Roman looked annoyed. "We need to talk," he said.

Ollie and Jessie looked towards him. She sat down next to Ollie, and they both looked at Roman.

Roman sat on the sofa across from the married couple. "So you want me to stop seeing other girls," he said. It was part statement, part question.

Ollie nodded yes.

"If I stop seeing other girls, then I want to see Jessie more," Roman said. He was speaking to Ollie and ignoring Jessie.

"How much?" Ollie asked.

And the negotiation for Jessie had begun.

Roman shrugged. "Alisha controls my life," he said. "She tells me when I can see my kids. So when I have an open night, I should get priority with Jessie. I think that's only fair."

"At most 3 times a week," Ollie said. "You're not going to be with her more nights than me."

Roman shrugged his agreement. Three nights a week with Jessie was a lot better than how it was now.

Jessie sat next to Ollie, feeling numb. *They're treating me like an object. Like a piece of meat. They're not even asking what I want,* she thought to herself.

She wanted to be a strong woman, she *was* a strong woman, she felt women were equals with men. But at that moment, the submissive part of her was coming out. She was in major sub-space. She hated – *but loved too* – the way they were treating her. Her pussy ached. She was dying to be fucked.

"When she's with me, she's with me," Roman demanded.

"Fine," Ollie said with a shrug. He expected as much.

"Don't say yes until you know what that means," Roman warned. "When Jessie's with me, you're the platonic friend. You get nothing from her. You can watch us and jerk off if you want, but you get nothing from her."

"Okay, I get it," Ollie said.

"Like right now," Roman said, motioning at Jessie sitting next to her husband. "Once we agree to it, if it's my night, Jessie would be sitting with me, not you."

Ollie hesitated before answering. When she was with Roman, sometimes he needed some of Jessie's attention to make it through the night. He could deal without sexual contact until after Roman was gone. But to not get a kiss or a hug, to get no affection at all, that would be hard.

Still, that kind of denial pushed Ollie's cuckold buttons. With mixed feelings, he nodded his agreement to Roman.

Roman wasn't done. "On my nights, Jessie sleeps with me," he demanded.

"No," Ollie said immediately.

"It's only fair Ollie," Roman said in reasonable tone. "You want me to stop seeing other girls. And why does it matter anyway? You're traveling all the time."

Ollie considered for long moments. Then he said, "Okay. But only when I'm away. And you only spend evenings together. After work ends. And then in the morning, she leaves. I don't want her spending days with you."

Roman gave Ollie a hard glare. But eventually he nodded his head in agreement.

Jessie hugged Ollie's arm and leaned into him. She loved this! Her two men – *her* two men – were fighting over her. They were negotiating their rights to her body. And they were ignoring her completely. She had no say. She was powerless. It was like she was a sex slave.

Jessie was so aroused!

"One more thing," Roman said. "When I'm with Jessie, she's with me right? So I don't want her wearing her wedding ring."

"No way," Ollie said shaking his head. "Jessie's my wife. She's always my wife, even when she's with you. So she wears her wedding ring. That's non-negotiable."

Roman and Ollie glared at each other for long moments. Finally Roman said, "Fine. But then she wears my ring too."

"What ring?"

"I have something in mind. It's a ring. And she'll wear my ring all the time. Just like your wedding ring. She'll wear both all the time."

Ollie considered and eventually shrugged. He said, "Okay."

Then Roman pushed for more, saying, "But she takes off her engagement ring. She wears your wedding ring, and the ring I give her. That's fair. One ring each."

Ollie glared at Roman for long moments. Then, eventually, he nodded his agreement.

With the rules set, Roman got up and held his hand for Jessie. She took it as she stood up. Roman put his arm around Jessie's waist and led her to the bedroom.

Jessie didn't look back at Ollie as Roman led her away. Under the new rules, she wasn't allowed to.

Ollie took a deep breath when they were gone. He was naturally a shy and non-confrontation person, so he was proud of himself for standing up to Roman. But still, he wondered how much he had given up. Jessie was his wife, she belonged to him. Yet, he had just given rights to Jessie to Roman. A lot of rights.

Still, his cock was incredibly hard. The jealousy and despair he felt – the angst – they were like gasoline thrown on the burning flames of his cuckold lust. He was so excited his body was shaking.

Ollie waited long moments, trying to collect himself, trying to stop his body from shaking, trying to stop his heart from pounding. Then he quietly went into the bedroom.

They were on the bed. Roman was naked. Jessie was naked too, except she still wore the black thigh high stockings and *So Kate* high heels.

They were kissing and fondling each other. Ollie watched as Roman got on top. Jessie opened her legs for him.

As they continued to kiss, Roman pushed his cock into Jessie. She moaned at the penetration. Soon she was impaled with his manhood.

Ollie couldn't hold back any longer. He sat down in the chair across from the bed and took out his cock. He began to slowly stroke himself, edging himself, not wanting to cum too fast.

Roman adjusted his angle of penetration with each thrust. Ollie had seen this before. Roman was searching for Jessie's g-spot.

Roman knew he found it when Jessie let out a soulful moan. Then he locked into that angle, fucking her deep and slow, rubbing against both her clit and g-spot with every in and out thrust.

Roman kissed Jessie as he fucked her, and she kissed him back, wrapping her arms around his neck to hug him close. Locked in that embrace, kissing while Roman fucked her deep and slow, it looked like they were making love rather than fucking.

This sight made Ollie's heart ache. It was a punch to his gut. The angst was so painful. Yet, so delicious too.

They fucked like that for long minutes. At some point, Roman put Jessie's legs over his shoulders. Then she was cumming, clitoral and g-spot orgasms rocking her young, tight body. Jessie cried out and her legs shook, throwing the high heels from her feet. Ollie watched Jessie's pretty toes – still in the black stockings – curl as massive orgasmic pleasure flooded her sexy body.

Ollie came at that moment, shooting his cum all over his hand. Then the sadness and angst of seeing his wife with another man –

making love to that man—overtook him, and he staggered from the master bedroom to the guest bedroom. He collapsed onto the bed. Soon after he passed out from weariness and the Highland Park scotch he'd drank earlier.

———————●———————

When Ollie woke up, the sunlight was streaming into his eyes. He was disoriented, and it took him a moment to remember what happened the night before. And what he agreed to. But then he remembered.

He wore boxers but was otherwise naked. He staggered from the guest bedroom to the kitchen, partially hungover, partially despondent.

He stopped in his tracks at what he saw.

An unfinished breakfast was on the table. Half full coffee cups. Half-eaten scrambled eggs and toast.

Roman was naked, sitting in the chair.

Jessie was wearing a man's shirt – Roman's shirt from last night – and it was unbuttoned. She sat in Roman's lap, straddling his hips. She had her arms around Roman's neck, kissing him.

Jessie was moving up and down. She was slowly fucking Roman.

Ollie was frozen. Almost on its own volition, his hand moved inside his boxers. He began to stroke himself as he watched his wife kiss and fuck her lover.

Jessie stopped kissing Roman. Looking into his face and still rocking on his cock, she caressed his body. His muscular arms and ripped chest. Her eyes were heavy with lust.

Ollie heard his wife whispered, "You have the most amazing body."

It was another dagger to Ollie's heart. Jessie had never said those words to him. Not in all their years together.

Roman's hand was inside his open shirt that Jessie wore, caressing her slim, sexy body. He ran his fingertips over her back, her sides, her breasts. Jessie moaned as he fondled her tits and thumbed her nipples. "I love the way you touch me," Jessie said. It was another dagger to Ollie's heart.

"You have to wear the wig again," Roman told Jessie as she slowly rode his cock. They were both speaking quietly.

"You like how I looked?" she asked.

"You looked so hot," Roman answered. "You have to wear it again."

"I will," Jessie said. She wrapped her arms around Roman's neck again and they kissed.

Moments later, Jessie came. She buried her head into Roman's shoulder to muffle her moans.

Not soon after, Roman quietly groaned "I'm cumming."

Jessie quickly pulled off Roman and got onto her knees. She pulled off the condom and swallowed the top of Roman's cock into her mouth. She used both hands to rapidly stroke him to completion. Ollie watched his wife's jaw and throat muscles work frantically to swallow all of Roman's huge ejaculation.

Then Jessie was wiping her lips with the back of her hand, and she and Roman giggled. They sounded like giddy teenagers who had just done something naughty and gotten away with it.

Only then did Jessie turn her head and see her husband watching them.

"Oh, Ollie baby ...," Jessie said, her voice trailing off. Her eyes lowered to his crotch. Ollie's hand was still in his boxers. There was a wet spot in his boxers, from where he came.

"Roman," Ollie said as he pulled his hand from his boxers and reached for a paper towel. "Leave."

Roman stared at Ollie for a long moment. Then he got up and retrieved his clothes from the master bedroom.

"Wait, here," Jessie said. She took off Roman's shirt and handed it to him.

Jessie moved to her husband and hugged him. She said, "I'm sorry. I thought you were sleeping. We were trying to be quiet."

Ollie couldn't respond. "*We* used to be you and me," he thought to himself. "When did *we* become you and Roman?"

Ollie was speechless. It hurt too much to say anything.

After a few minutes, Roman emerged from the bedroom. He gave Jessie a look then moved towards the door.

"Would it be alright if I said goodbye to him?" Jessie asked her husband. Ollie reluctantly nodded his head yes. Then he reached for a blanket they used when watching TV. "Put this on," he said as he wrapped the blanket around Jessie's naked body.

Ollie knew it was a stupid gesture, given what they'd just been doing. But he didn't want his wife naked as she said goodbye to Roman.

The way their apartment was laid out, Ollie couldn't see Jessie and Roman at the door. But he could hear them, and he heard whispers, and then kissing. Then the door opened and closed. Then Jessie was back.

She dropped the blanket onto the floor. Then she hugged Ollie with her naked body.

"Come here baby," Jessie said, and she began leading Ollie to the guest bedroom. But Ollie steered her to the master bedroom. He needed to see it. He was drawn to it like a moth to a roaring fire.

Their bedroom reeked of sex. The sheets and blankets were thrown off the bed. Most of the pillows were on the floor. There were multiple wet spots in the mattress.

"Did you get any sleep?" Ollie joked as his eyes took in the sex playroom that used to be their master bedroom.

Jessie gave him a weak smile. "I went to you last night," she said. "In the guest room. But you were sleeping."

Ollie looked at her and nodded.

"It's a little chilly," she said as she put her robe on. Ollie continued to look at her. He couldn't help thinking "*you weren't cold a minute ago when you were riding his cock.*"

"I'll be right back," Jessie said. "I want to clean up a little bit."

She moved towards the bathroom. Halfway there, she stopped when he said, "I don't like seeing you in his shirt."

"Yes, I get it, I'm sorry," Jessie said.

"But I guess when you're with him, you're his, so I can't do anything about it," Ollie said bitterly.

"Ollie, baby, I'll be right back," Jessie said gently. She disappeared into the bathroom. Ollie heard her brushing her teeth, swirling mouthwash.

"*How considerate,*" Ollie thought to himself. "*Since he just came in her mouth.*"

A few moments later, Jessie was back. She slipped the robe off her shoulders. Ollie looked at his wife's naked body. She looked the same as before. Petite and slim, yet with sexy curves that were perfect for her size. Very tight. Very sexy.

Ollie was hard, his cock denting the boxers, even though he'd just cum a moment ago. Jessie saw it and said "Do you want to stay here? Or go into the guest room?"

Ollie answered by pulling Jessie into his arms and kissing her. He pushed his tongue into her mouth, not wanting, *but wanting*, to taste any remnants of Roman's cum in her mouth.

Ollie pushed Jessie onto the bed and she opened her legs for him. He tugged off the boxers and then guided his hard cock to her pussy. He pushed into her. He got balls deep with practically no resistance.

"Fuck you're so loose!" he growled. "His big cock really stretched you!"

"Roman talked about ruining Alisha's body," Jessie said. She knew her husband would want to hear this.

"What?"

"He said Alisha used to be really hot," Jessie said. "But she's not anymore. Not after being pregnant 3 times. He said he got the best years of Alisha. Her new boyfriend's getting his leftovers."

"Oh god Jessie!" Ollie moaned excitedly. "Did he say he wanted to do that to you?"

"No but, I'll be seeing him more now. You agreed to it," Jessie said. "He'll be fucking me more with his big cock. He's going to stretch my pussy Ollie. I'm warning you baby. Roman's going to ruin my pussy for your little cock."

"Oh fuck!!!" Ollie cried and he came, jack-rabbiting his cock into Jessie's well used pussy. He wasn't wearing a condom so he shot his sperm into her unprotected, fertile womb.

Afterwards they held each other tight. With Jessie's head buried in his chest, Ollie said "I hope I just got you pregnant. So you'll stop seeing him."

Jessie raised her head. She got on an elbow and looked at her husband. "If you want me to stop seeing him, then why do you want him to stop seeing other girls? Why'd you agree to let him see me more?"

"I don't know," Ollie said with a weak smile. "I don't get myself. My fantasies. I don't understand them."

Jessie nodded. She understood. She didn't understand her fantasies either.

"What are we going to do Ollie?" she asked. "Do you really want me to see Roman more?"

"I don't know," Ollie said. "But tell me what happened last night."

Jessie told Ollie everything. She stroked his cock as she did, and he came twice before she finally got to the end.

Ollie, like Jessie, was concerned people would recognize her as the girl who got fucked last night in the HL23, and got her pretty face splattered with cum.

They searched the internet for videos and pictures. They finally found a site called "HL23 – Sex Tapes of the Rich and (*now they are*) Infamous."

And there they were. Pictures and videos of Jessie getting fucked by Roman against the big window in unit 6 of HL23.

The married couple freaked at first, but they calmed down as they studied the pictures and watched the videos. The wig did disguise Jessie's appearance. And while you could tell that the girl getting fucked was pretty, you couldn't make out her features. While the apartment windows seemed crystal clear from the inside, they must have been covered in a film that slightly distorted the view from the outside.

With the fear of Jessie being outed taken care of, Ollie allowed his lusts take over. The pictures and videos were incredibly hot.

Ollie made Jessie put on the wig. He was startled to see her wearing it. She looked like a different person. She was still very beautiful, but with blonde hair she looked young, sweet and innocent. With short black hair, she looked older, sophisticated and sassy.

Ollie fucked his wife. As he fucked her, he hissed "If Roman can fuck you when you're my blonde wife, I'll fuck you when you're his brunette girlfriend."

Afterwards, Ollie was overcome with despair. The angst was more pronounced now, since his sexual desires were sated after cumming so many times in so short a time.

Jessie in the wig did not look like his wife. Where was her long blonde hair? The silky golden locks he loved to run his fingers through.

Jessie did not look like the girl he loved. She did not look like the girl he cherished, the person he loved more than anyone in the world.

He remembered when they were first dating. When they got serious. Jessie had a thin, trimmed landing strip above her sweet looking pussy. It was blonde, just like the hair on her head. Jessie was bare everywhere else, completely hairless, except for that landing strip and the blonde hair on her hair.

Ollie asked Jessie to shave the landing strip off. He wanted her to be completely bare.

Jessie said no. Back then, she told him if she was completely bare, it would make her feel like a teenager again, and she told Ollie that she was trying to grow up and become more mature. Of course, Ollie respected and supported her decision.

From that day until now, Jessie often teased him, saying that by keeping a little landing strip, he would know she was a natural blonde. Ollie remembered grinning. He remembered grabbing her as she laughed, and they had wonderful, loving sex.

But with Jessie in the wig, with short black hair, it was like all those great memories never happened. And it made Ollie extremely sad.

Ollie made Jessie take the wig off. He said, "I hope I never see you wearing that again."

But he didn't tell her to stop seeing Roman.

CHAPTER 9

On Monday, Ollie went on another business trip. He wouldn't be back home until Thursday. Three nights away from home.

Jessie had a free pass to be with Roman all three nights, if she wanted. It scared him, but excited him too.

He cursed all the traveling he had to do. But he had to travel for work. If he told his boss he wanted to stop, he'd probably be let go by the end of the week.

<hr />

Roman didn't waste any time. He called Jessie and asked her out for Monday night. "Stay over," he said. "Bring some clothes and you can leave from my place for work tomorrow."

"Roman – I mean, Romes – it's not that easy. You don't have a garage, and I know people in your neighborhood. What if they see my car there?"

"So I'll stay over at your place," Roman said. "What's your size?"

"What?"

"What's your panty size? I want to get you some."

"*Oooookay*," Jessie said with a laugh. Roman laughed too.

"So what's your size?" he asked again, the laugh still in his voice.

"Um ... 0 mostly," Jessie said.

Roman grinned into the phone. "You are a *little* submissive slut, aren't you?" he joked.

"Romes, god," Jessie said, looking nervously around her office. She was speaking in a low voice, but if any of her co-workers found out she was having an affair – especially Harper or Sophie – it would seriously make her life shitty.

"So you want my bra size too?" Jessie asked, half joking. Although she thought he would want to get her a matching bra/panty set.

"Nope," Roman said taking her question seriously. "You don't wear bras when you're with me."

"Oh my god," Jessie said with a laugh.

"I mean it," Roman said, but he had a laugh in his voice too.

"Okay, whatever," Jessie said grinning. "But that'll affect what top I wear, you know. I mean, there's sexy, and there's obscene."

Then she said, "You know how you want me to wear a ring?"

"My ring," he corrected. "So?"

"Ollie bought my engagement ring when he was just out of college. He didn't have much money. And he wasn't drafted by the NFL."

"I got cut after my first year," he reminded her.

"You were still drafted!" Jessie said with a laugh. "I mean, get real."

"Okay, whatever -—so?"

"So, I don't want you to buy me something expensive," Jessie said. "Whatever you get me, it can't be better than my engagement ring."

"At some point, if I'm giving up other girls, and you're my *girlfriend*—," Roman said, emphasizing "girlfriend" like he was putting air quotes around it, "—then you have to stop worrying about Ollie so much and worry about me. What am I getting out of this?"

"I'm Ollie's wife, and he's letting you have sex with me," Jessie whispered into the phone. "He's giving me to you three times a week. He's letting us date. He's letting me sleep with you. I think you're getting a lot."

"And you don't want that too?" Roman said, frowning into the phone.

"Of course, I want that," Jessie whispered. "That's why I'm freaking talking to you about this."

In an even lower voice, she said "I want you to fuck me. Make me do things, like at HL23. But don't you see? You're getting a lot. And

I love Ollie. Just cause I'm crushing on you doesn't mean I don't love him."

"Okay, okay, I get it," Roman said, relenting. It felt good to hear her say again she was crushing on him. And to hear her admit she wanted him to take charge and do things to her. He knew this was something she couldn't get from her husband.

"Anyway, it doesn't matter," he said. "I know the ring I'm giving you. And it doesn't look like an engagement ring so you don't have to worry about it."

Jessie couldn't help smiling. "What is it?" she asked, intrigued.

"Oh, so now you want to know?" Roman said with playful sarcasm.

"Of course I do. I'm a girl, remember?"

"Let me tell you Jessie, I know you're a girl," Roman joked, and they both laughed.

"I'll give the ring to you tonight," he said. "Then you never take it off."

"Never?" Jessie teased.

"Do you ever take off your ring?"

"Sometimes I take off my engagement ring," Jessie said. "If I'm working out, or like, gardening. But I never take off my wedding ring. Unless I'm cleaning it."

"Then you don't take off my ring unless you're cleaning it. Okay?"

"Okay," Jessie said. She was charmed and flattered by Roman's insistence and felt incredibly close to him at that moment. She was crushing big time on him. She knew it was dangerous, but she decided to just go with it. After all, that's what Ollie wanted too.

"Dress sexy tonight," Roman told her. "Do you have a dress that buttons up the front? That shows your legs?"

"I have one. It's sort of old. It's not super short," Jessie said. "It's above my knees though."

Jessie could practically hear Roman's disapproval over the phone. But he eventually said, "Okay, that's good enough. Wear Stockings. And high heels," Roman told her. "And like I said. No bra."

"I got it master," Jessie joked.

"I am your master," Roman joked back. Jessie laughed.

"And Jessie?"

"Yeah?"

"Put on the wig."

<hr>

Roman arrived to Jessie looking like a short haired brunette. He took a moment to look at her. "Fuck you're beautiful," he gushed. Jessie couldn't help smiling at his compliment.

Jessie's braless nipples were denting her dress. He reached out and thumb one. "Very nice," he said.

"I'm glad you approve," Jessie said with a laugh. But her cheeks flushed as he touched her. He continued to thumb her nipple for long moments. Jessie began to breath harder. The idea of skipping dinner and just going to bed passed through her pretty head.

Roman pulled his hand away. "Forgot to take that off?" he asked, gesturing to Jessie's left hand.

Her engagement ring. She *had* forgotten about that part of the agreement.

"Is it really that important?" she asked.

"Take it off Jessie," Roman ordered, his voice hard.

She looked at him for a moment, but wasn't able to meet his intensity. With her right hand, she slid her engagement ring off. She put it in the drawer of the side table where she knew it would be safe.

Her left hand suddenly felt wrong. It wasn't unusual for her to take off her engagement ring for short periods of time. But she always wore both her rings – her engagement and wedding rings – when going out, like she was about to do now.

But she was going out with Roman, not Ollie. And the way he was ordering her around ... commanding her ... it was a side of him she was seeing more and more of.

And Jessie liked it.

"This is for you," Roman said, handing Jessie a small box. It was from *La Perla*. Jessie knew the famous lingerie store. She went to the one on Madison Avenue sometimes when she wanted something special.

She opened and looked into the box. Inside were neatly folded panties and garter belts. They were all lace and mostly brown, black and green.

"I noticed most of your lingerie is pink, red and white," Roman said.

Jessie nodded. "Ollie's favorite colors on me," she said. Her husband liked her to look sweet and innocent. And young. He sometimes joked he liked her looking like she was barely legal.

"Mine are brown, black and green," Roman told her.

"I see that," Jessie said with a half laugh, still looking into the box.

"What I buy you, don't wear for Ollie," Roman told her.

Jessie looked at Roman. Once again, he was commanding her. This time, to deny her husband something. But then, what he wanted wasn't unreasonable. Roman had bought them for her after all. And Ollie probably wouldn't want her to wear for him anything Roman bought her anyways.

"Put one of the panties on," Roman told her.

Jessie reached inside the box. Only then did she realize all the panties were g-strings. Normally she wore thongs.

"Um, really?" she said, holding up one of the g-strings. It was emerald green. There wasn't much to it. Just thin strings – *very* thin—with a tiny triangle in the front. It was barely anything.

"Your ass is too tight and sexy for thongs," Roman said. "Only g-strings for you when you're with me. Put one on."

Jessie began moving towards the bedroom to put the panties on. Roman stopped her by saying, "No. Right here. I want to watch you."

Jessie hesitated. It was hard enough to change panties when dressed, especially with the tight dress she was wearing, and with her heels on. She didn't really want an audience. But the way he was ordering her around ... like he owned her body ... she found it arousing.

Jessie tugged up her dress, exposing her long, shapely legs. She was wearing black thigh high stockings and *Jimmy Choo* high heels.

Jessie curled her thumbs into her thong panties and pulled them down her stockinged legs. She worked them past the pointy stilettos of the Jimmy Choos. She was about to put the emerald green g-string on when Roman told her to stop.

"Sit on the sofa," he commanded. "Keep your skirt up."

Jessie stared at him for a moment. Then she did as he said.

Roman sat next to her on the sofa. He looked down at her legs. She was completely exposed from the waist down.

Roman caressed the heavy lace of her stocking tops. "You wore these for me?" he asked, referring to the thigh highs.

"Yes," Jessie said. It was true. She had thought of him as she dressed, wanting to wear things that he liked. Or what he asked her to wear, like the button up dress she was wearing.

She didn't say she also usually wore stockings for Ollie too, when they went out. Both men were into legs, and Jessie knew how to use her legs for the pleasure of her man (or, at the moment, her two men). She had always been slim and leggy and, even as a young girl, had noticed men admiring her legs. So she had years of experience learning how to tease and attract men with her legs.

"You haven't shaved this off yet," Roman said as he teasingly ran his fingertip lightly over the thin trimmed landing strip just above her clit. Other than the landing strip, she kept herself completely bare, the only hair on her sexy body being her long blonde hair on her pretty head.

Jessie flushed as he touched her so close to her most intimate parts.
"No Romes. I told you. I don't want to look like a teenager," Jessie said.
"And it reminds Ollie I'm a natural blonde."

Roman frown at her. He didn't want to hear about Ollie when she
was with him. Reading his thoughts, Jessie said "You're the one who
brought it up."

"So how did Ollie like all those people watching me fuck you?" he
asked spitefully.

"You know there's a website for HL23 sex videos?" Jessie asked.

"Of course I know," Roman said with a laugh. "There are a few
websites. It's my friend's apartment and he's wild. He's on a few of those
videos. That's why he put film on the outside of the windows."

"It would've been nice to know that," Jessie said sourly.

"I wanted to see your reaction," Roman told her. "You liked being
watched. It got you hot."

"I was mortified Romes," Jessie said. "All those people watching me.
And if people had recognized me, I'd be in such shit."

"For someone who was mortified, you came really hard," Roman
joked. He was stroking her landing strip again. "And I think the risk of
people finding out you're a submissively little slut gets you hot too."

Roman's words reminded her what Ollie said. *We both get off on
the risk.*

Roman's fingertips moved to the sliver of bare skin between her
landing strip and clit. He was softly caressing circles over that sensitive
flesh, and it was driving her crazy.

"Fuck me," she told him. Her face was flushed. She looked beyond
aroused.

"We'll be late for dinner," Roman said with a grin.

"I don't care," Jessie said.

Roman laughed. Then he surprised her. He got down on his knees
and parted her legs. He pulled her forward so her ass was barely on the
sofa. Then he lowered his head and went down on her.

Jessie was shocked. Roman had never gone down on her before, except for minor foreplay here and there.

She moaned as he licked up her slit, and then twirled his tongue over her slit. Roman wasn't as good as Ollie. No one was as good as her husband at eating pussy. But Jessie was already so aroused, she knew she would orgasm in moments if he licked her clit.

Jessie gripped the edges of the sofa cushions and opened her legs wider, the stilettos of the Jimmy Choos scaping as she slid them across the hardwood floor. "Oh god, Romes, feels so good, so good," she moaned.

Then Roman pushed a finger into her wet pussy while licking her clit. He pushed in another. Jessie cried out. She was seconds from cumming.

"Don't stop, shit, don't stop, I'm almost there!" Jessie begged.

Then abruptly Roman withdrew his tongue from Jessie's clit. He pulled out his fingers. And he stood up.

"No, Roman, what?" Jessie cried, not understanding.

"I want you to call me Romes."

"Okay, whatever, Romes!" Jessie cried out in frustration. "Why'd you stop? I'm almost there!"

"Because you don't say no to me," Roman told her. He tossed the emerald green g-string at her. "Put this on."

Jessie stared at him incredulously. She couldn't believe it! She was right there! Right there!

Feeling sexually frustrated, she stood up. Her knees were weak and she was unsteady in the Jimmy Choos.

The dress was still around her waist. She stepped into the g-string and pulled it up her long stockinged legs. The tiny triangle in front barely covered her thin trimmed landing strip.

"When you shave it off, I'll buy you g's that are all strings," Roman promised.

"I'll never shave it off for you!" Jessie screamed.

"Then maybe I won't let you cum all night," Roman warmed.

Jessie immediately surrendered. *"No ... no,"* she thought to herself. She needed to cum! She needed Roman to make her cum!

"Romes, baby, I told you why I'm not shaving it off," Jessie said in a panicked voice. "And anyways, if I won't shave it off for Ollie, I can't shave it off for you. You understand that, don't you?"

Roman glared at her but didn't push it any further. But maybe as punishment, he said, "Our reservation's at Daniel." He was referring to the famous NYC French restaurant.

"Romes, baby, we can't," Jessie said cautiously. She didn't want to say no to him again, but this wasn't possible. "Our friends go there. My co-workers go there. Ollie's too. I'll know people there for sure."

"Put on heavier makeup," Roman told her with finality. "That plus the wig, no one will recognize you."

When Jessie hesitated, his tone turned reasonable. "Look, just try it," he said. "If you're still worried after putting on more make up, we'll go someplace else."

Jessie realized she couldn't argue with that. As she moved towards the bedroom where she kept her makeup, he said "Something darker. You're a brunette now. Darker makeup looks better on brunettes."

Jessie looked at Roman for a long moment. Then she nodded her head and continued on to her bedroom.

Jessie had many brunette friends, so she knew how to adjust her makeup as Roman wanted. She applied a darker, brownish blush, eyeshadow, eyeliner and mascara. She applied the makeup heavier than she usually wore, to further the disguise. Lastly, she wiped off the pinkish lipstick she normally wore, and brushed on brownish lipstick that had a moist sheen to it.

When she was done, she looked at herself in the mirror. She was shocked. The dark, heavier makeup combined with the short black hair made her look like a different person. She practically didn't recognize herself.

Jessie rejoined Roman in the TV room. "Okay, you're right. I'll go to Daniel," she told him. "But let's get a table in the back. Please. Okay?"

Roman nodded, but he'd barely heard her words. He was staring at her. Short black hair and dark makeup. "God Jessie, you're so beautiful," he enthused admiringly, his demeanor softening from just moments ago. "You take my breath away."

Even though she was still irritated with him, Jessie couldn't help smiling.

———⟡———

I n the taxi, Roman caressed Jessie's wrist like he'd done the other day. She was already aroused, and his caressed just made her hotter. "Why are you doing this to me?" she asked helplessly through heavy breathing.

"What, this?" Roman teased as he moved his hand up from her wrist, and used his fingertips to lightly caress her neck just below her ear.

Jessie gritted her teeth to stifle a moan. "Romes, you're freaking driving me crazy," she said, feeling even more aroused and sexually frustrated. Hating herself for sounding so weak, she asked, "You won't really not let me cum, will you?"

"Be a good girl Jessie, and I'll get you off," Roman promised. "You know what it means to be a good girl?"

Jessie knew. "To be your little submissive slut," she whispered.

"Are you my little submissive slut?" he asked.

"Yes," Jessie said.

"Say the whole thing," Roman commanded.

Jessie's cheeks flushed, feeling so submissive and humiliated. She whispered, "I'm your little submissive slut."

Roman grinned.

He moved closer and kissed her. Jessie immediately parted her lips, and he pushed in his tongue. Then he kissed down her neck, making her moan.

She wanted to scream!

He was driving her crazy! She needed release! She needed an orgasm!

She needed fucked!

"I'll be okay with it if you, you know, wanted to wall fuck me between the appetizers and entrées," she said. She was only half joking.

Roman laughed. Then, getting serious, he said "No Jessie. I've got plans for your body."

Jessie's eyes went wide. The way he said "your body" instead of "you" made her shudder. It made her feel like he was objectifying her, treating her not as a person, not as an equal, but as a sex toy, as a thing whose only use was to be fucked and to give pleasure to men. Jessie was a feminist, she believed in equal rights for women, but at that moment, she was so *freaking* turned on!

"Anyway, what about your friends?" Roman asked.

"What?" Jessie said, not understanding.

"All those people you know who are in Daniel," Roman said. "What if they see you walking out into the alley with me? What if some of them watch me fuck you?"

"I'm wearing my disguise," Jessie said.

"What if I say your name while I'm fucking you?"

"You wouldn't do that."

Roman gave her a look as to say *don't be too sure of that.* Then he said, "You know what's another little known erogenous zone?"

"What?" Jessie asked, momentarily confused by the abrupt change of subject.

"The soles of your feet," Roman said.

"Seriously? That tickles," Jessie said.

"Does this tickle?" Roman said as he caressed her wrist again. "Or turn you on?"

"Turn me on," Jessie said honestly.

"You see? It's all how you do it. And when you do it. Context matters."

Jessie was breathing hard and wet between her legs as the taxi finally arrived at Daniel.

Inside Daniel, at their request, the hostess seated them in a side dining room. Their table was surrounded by others, but at least they avoided the crowded main dining room. As she feared, Jessie saw a few people she knew, but they didn't seem to recognize her with the short black hair and the darker, heavier makeup. She breathed a sigh of relief.

Daniel was known for its amazing wine list in addition to its wonderful French food. Roman ordered an expensive Bordeaux. He was more of a beer man, but he wanted to treat Jessie who loved wine.

As they sipped their wines, Roman reached into his pocket and pulled out a ring. He gave it to Jessie.

Jessie looked at it. The ring was a simple gold band, like a wedding ring. Except along the top of the ring were the scripted letters "*We Are #44.*"

As a lifelong Penn State football fan, Jessica recognized this immediately. "This is a Penn State football ring?" she asked. The *We Are* was the Penn State chant: *We Are – Penn State!*

Roman nodded and said "It's my ring. 44 was my number. All the seniors got them at our last home game."

"But, this is too small for you," Jessie said. "It's a woman's ring."

Roman nodded again. He said, "It's my mom's ring. We were allowed to buy rings for our parents. So I bought my mom and dad rings. You know – for having to put up with me being such an ass growing up."

Jessie handed the ring back to him. "Romes, I can't take this from your mother," she said.

"She died a few years ago," Roman told her. "My dad gave it to me when she died."

"Oh my god, Romes, I'm so sorry," Jessie said. "But now I really can't take it."

"You and me, it's temporary, I get that," Roman said. "When it's over, you can give it back to me. Right now though, I *want* you to wear it. It'll make me feel good. You're special to me Jessie." With a grin, he joked, "Like I said, you're a great rebound girlfriend."

Jessie gave a half laugh at his joke. She was incredibly flattered, and charmed. "Well, okay then," she said, smiling wide as if she was back in grade school and the boy she liked just asked her to go steady. Which sort of this was.

In fact, Jessie remembered her conversation with Ollie, when they joked about Roman giving her his high school ring since they were going steady. This ring was kind of like that, except it was his college ring, not high school.

"Here, let me put it on you," Roman said. Still smiling, Jessie held up her right hand.

"No, the other one," Roman said. Before she could object, he took her left hand and slid off her wedding ring. He put her wedding ring on the table, then slid his #44 ring onto her wedding ring finger. "Perfect fit," he said.

"Romes, this isn't what Ollie agreed to," she said looking doubtful. "I take off my engagement ring and wear your ring, but I wear my wedding ring too."

"So go ahead, put it back on," Roman said motioning to Ollie's wedding ring on the table. "Put it on your right hand."

"Romes ...," Jessie began uncertainly.

"When you're not with me, you switch the rings," Roman said. "Easy. We all win."

Jessie wasn't sure Ollie was winning, not with his wedding ring relegated to her right hand, especially with Roman's #44 ring taking its place on her wedding ring finger. But Roman was so dominate and commanding, and she felt so submissive to him.

Jessie slid her wedding ring – Ollie's ring – on the ring finger of her right hand.

"There you go. You're being a good girl," Roman said, like an adult to a child. "My good little submissive slut."

Jessie shuddered at his words. The more she was around him, the more she was drawn to him. She felt so feminine to his masculinity. So submissive to his domination.

"What now?" Jessie asked in a low soft voice.

Roman wrapped his hand behind her neck. He pulled her to him. And he kissed her.

Even though they were in public, even though people she knew where in the very next room, Jessie didn't resist. She let Roman kiss her. She surrendered to him.

"Let's go," Roman ordered, throwing some bills on the table.

"Yes, let's go," Jessie agreed breathlessly. *God, she wanted him so bad!*

CHAPTER 10

A taxi was waiting outside Daniel. Roman dropped two fifties on the driver's lap and said "drive around Central Park."

Roman was all over Jessie, kissing and caressing her. Jessie urgently kissed and caressed him back.

Jessie had Roman's shirt open, and was kissing and caressing his muscular chest. His well defined pecs and abs turned her on so much!

Somehow in the tight confides of the taxi, Roman maneuvered Jessie so she lay on top of him, with her back on his front. With her shoulders and head turned, they were still passionately kissing. And in this position, Roman was running his hands up and down the front of her body.

Jessie knew the taxi driver was probably watching in the rear view mirror. At that moment, she was beyond caring. Her body screamed for release! And Roman was right, she liked being watched, like at the High Line. Ollie was right too. The danger excited her.

At some point, Jessie realized the taxi was no longer moving. They were still in Central Park, but not on the road. Instead, they were parked among a cluster of tall, thick evergreen trees. It was pitch black outside, although lights from the dashboard illuminated the inside of the taxi.

Then Jessie realized something else. There was someone in the backseat with them! It was the taxi driver!

Jessie looked at his face and she recognized him. It was Amir!

"Hello Miss Jessie," Amir said with a malicious, toothy grin. He had a heavy Arabic accent. "I think you remember me, yes?"

Alarms went off in Jessie head. What was he doing here?

Jessie realized her feet were in Amir's lap. She tried to move away, but Roman held her shoulders so she couldn't move. "Calm down Jessie," he said. "I called Amir. I told you I had plans for your body tonight."

Holding her tight, Roman planted his lips on hers. He kissed her hard, forcing his tongue into her mouth.

Jessie shrugged but she couldn't move. Roman was holding her shoulders. And now Amir was holding her ankles. She was completely helpless!

Jessie felt Amir move his hand up her leg. With his other hand he continued to hold both of her ankles.

"You have very nice legs," Amir said with that thick accent, as he caressed from her ankles to her thighs. Jessie felt violated as Amir felt her up. She tried to pull away again but both men held her tight.

Roman was kissing her neck again. "Calm down Jessie," he told her again. "Me and Amir are just going to have a little fun with your sexy body."

"Nooooo," Jessie whined. She remembered how Roman and Alisha had threesomes. Was he going to let Amir fuck her?

Amir took off one of her heels, tossing the expensive Jimmy Choos onto the floor.

"You have very pretty feet Miss Jessie," Amir said in his thick accent. Amir caressed the top of her stockinged covered feet. His fingers were rough and callused from hard labor, and they scratched the delicate silk of her stockings.

Then Amir caressed his fingertips along the soles of her feet. Jessie sucked in her breath at the sensations. Roman hissed into her ear, "I knew you'd love it!"

Roman began unbuttoning the front of her dress. Jessie tried to resist but she was powerless with his strong arms pinning her sides.

"You wanna see her tits Amir?" Roman asked as he continued unbuttoning the front of her dress. Now Jessie understood why he told her to wear this dress. He planned this!

"Noooooo," Jessie whined as she struggled again. Roman pressed her sides harder with his elbows, preventing her from moving.

"Stop fighting Jessie," he said with a taunting grin. "Or I won't let you cum."

His words made heat rise to her pretty face, and shivers ran down her young tight body.

Roman kissed Jessie again to stop any further objections. As he stuck his tongue down her throat, he finished unbuttoning the front of Jessie's dress down to her waist. Then, while still pinning her body with his elbows, he used his hands to open the front of her dress wide.

Jessie chest was exposed to Amir's eyes. Her braless breasts were exposed to the Muslim's eyes.

Roman stopped kissing her so she could see Amir looking at her. He was staring hungrily at her small yet perfect little A cup breasts.

"Go ahead and touch her," Roman said, and again Jessie struggled to no avail.

"Romes, nooooo," Jessie whined. She tried to pull away from Amir but she was captive to the two men.

Amir cupped her tender breasts with his rough callused palms. When he rubbed her nipples, she couldn't help moaning.

"See Amir? See likes it," Roman said with a laugh.

Amir grinned at Roman, and then moved closer to Jessie so his pock marked face was closer to hers. He smelled of cigarettes and sweat. As he groped her tits, he ran the flat of his thick tongue up her face. Jessie cringed at the violation. Roman laughed and said, "She liked that. Do it again Amir." Amir grinned and sloppily licked her face again.

"Show Jessie your cock Amir," Roman said. He said hotly into her ear, "He told me he has a big cock. You like big cocks, don't you Jessie?"

Amir pulled back so Jessie could see more of his body. He was a big man with broad shoulders but with a paunchy gut.

Amir pulled down his pants. His cock was big, although not nearly as big as Roman's. It was dark like Amir's skin, and heavy veins ran up the sides. It was in a nest of coarse black pubic hair.

"You like my cock Miss Jessie?" Amir asked with a toothy grin. Jessie saw his teeth were stained from smoking. His gaze shifted from Jessie's pretty face to her bare breasts as he began stroking his hard shaft.

"You want him to fuck you Jessie?" Roman asked. "Amir's not as big as me, but bigger than Ollie."

Roman reached down. He grabbed the bottom of Jessie's skirt and pulled it up until it was around her waist. Amir hungrily feasted on her long shapely legs in the black thigh high stockings.

"Pull down her g-string Amir," Roman said.

"No Roman please ...," Jessie begged, again trying to wiggle away from Amir but going nowhere with Roman's muscular arms pinning her in place.

Amir ran his hands up Jessie's slim, beautiful legs. He grabbed the g-string – really nothing more than thin strings – and pulled it off. His eyes were now on her pussy, two thin lips pressed together, a shade darker than the surrounding white skin. Her lips glistened with moisture.

Roman used his knees to open Jessie's legs. Jessie felt her legs being opened and she struggled again. "Roman no ...," she begged.

But soon her legs were open. Amir had an even better view of Jessie's young, beautiful pussy. She was ripe to be taken. And with her legs open, Jessie felt even more vulnerable and violated.

Amir began stroking his cock again, his eyes fixed on Jessie's pussy.

Roman kissed along Jessie neck, just behind her ear, and she moaned. With one hand, he fondled one of her breasts. He moved his other hand down her body, over her flat tummy, to her pussy.

Roman began caressing Jessie's pussy with his fingertips. He used a light touch, and stayed away from her clit. His caresses aroused her even more, but they were not enough to make her cum.

"Tell Amir to fuck you," Roman said. He spoke in a calm reasonable voice that belied the intensity of the moment. "I know you want cock. Tell him to fuck you. He'll make you cum. Then I'll fuck you and make you cum more."

"No Romes, no," Jessie begged as she frantically shook her head no.

"You want fucked?" Roman asked.

"Yes! I wanted you to fuck me!" Jessie cried. Her body was desperate for her lover's cock! For release!

"Tell Amir to fuck you," Roman said again. "Or the only cock you'll get tonight is Ollie's."

Roman began tracing circles around Jessie's clit. He used a light touch, barely grazing her soft sensitive flesh. Then he scraped his fingertip lightly over her clit. He edged her along on the precipice of an orgasm, but denied her release.

"Romes, god, please .," Jessie begged. Her eyes were watering up with tears. "Don't make me. Please don't ...."

"Tell Amir to fuck you," Roman said again. "I know you, Jessie. You want to be forced."

"Then force me then!" Jessie said in anger and frustration. "If you know me so well! You tell Amir!"

"I *am* forcing you," Roman said in that same calm reasonable voice. "I'm forcing you to let Amir use your body. I'm forcing you to let him make you cum."

Jessie stared at Roman.

"Tell him Jessie."

"Don't make me Romes," she pleaded. There were tears in her eyes.

"Tell him," Roman ordered again, his voice hard.

Jessie hesitated for long moments. Finally, she looked at Amir. She nodded her head at him.

"That's not enough Jessie. You have to say the words. And use his name," Roman ordered.

"Fuck me Amir," Jessie whispered. Tears were running down her pretty cheeks. She had never felt so weak. Or submissive. Or humiliated.

Amir moved up between Jessie's open legs. His cock almost touched her pussy. Jessie couldn't look. She squeezed her eyes shut, preparing herself to be penetrated by the old Muslim man. He would be the second man (after Roman) to be inside her since she took her wedding vows. What will Ollie say when she told him?

But Amir made no move to push his cock into her. He just stared at her pretty face and sexy body and began jerking his cock again.

Roman pushed two fingers into Jessie's pussy. He began to finger fuck her hard and fast. He did the same to her clit, rubbing it hard and fast.

It was too much. She was too far gone. Jessie came. She screamed as a massive orgasm rocked her sexy body.

As her tight body quivered with orgasmic aftershocks, Amir began to frantically jerk himself off. With a thunderous cry, his body jerked and shuddered, and he orgasmed. Roman quickly pulled back his hand, and Amir pointed his spasming cock at Jessie's pussy and splashed his sperm all over Jessie's married clit and pussy lips.

———◉———

Amir drove them to Roman's house. Jessie rushed into his house with Roman following. As she ran, she held her dress closed as her hands had been too shaky in the taxi to re-button it.

Jessie looked back only to make sure Amir wasn't following. He remained in the taxi, his eyes following her every movement.

Inside his house, Roman was immediately on top of Jessie. Everyone had cum except him, and now it was his turn. To his credit though, he hurriedly rolled a condom down his cock before entering her.

Roman fucked her hard and fast. He didn't last long. Within moments he was cumming.

He pulled out and collapsed onto his back, panting. Jessie stared up at the ceiling. Roman pulled off the condom and threw it onto the floor. He'd clean up later.

After a few moments, Jessie moved off the bed. "I'm going home," she said. She reached for her phone to call an uBer.

"You're sleeping over," Roman said.

"You made that agreement with Ollie," Jessie told him. "But where I sleep is up to me."

"So why are you leaving?" he asked.

"Why the fuck do you think I'm leaving!" Jessie angrily cried.

"What we did tonight? You loved it," Roman said knowingly, so sure of himself.

"Fuck you Romes!" Jessie yelled.

"Think about it Jessie. What *really* happened tonight?" Roman said. He was using the calm reasonable voice again. "Amir saw your tits. He saw your pussy. He touched you a little. Come on Jessie. Was it that bad? You did more with dudes when you played your game with Ollie. Shit, I saw you almost get fucked. Remember?"

"I told you no!" Jessie screamed. "I told you to stop! And you held me! You wouldn't let me go!"

"And you loved it," Roman said. "Face it Jessie. With you, no doesn't mean no."

Jessie slapped Roman across the face. Hard.

Roman was silent for a moment. His cheek stung, but Jessie's hand hurt even worse.

Then he said in that calm, reasonable voice, "If you screamed in the taxi, like you're screaming now, then I would've stopped. I would've told Amir to fuck off."

Roman paused to let that sink in. Then he said, "Be honest with yourself Jessie. And with me. You loved it. You get off on being treated this way."

Jessie turned her face away in shame. Because she knew he was right. And it confused her. It scared her.

"Remember that time in the alley, when that dude was about to fuck you?" Roman asked. "What if things went bad? Where was Ollie? Now think about tonight. I was there to protect you if Amir tried to force himself on you."

"Don't you *dare* compare yourself to my husband!" Jessie angrily cried. "Ollie's my hero! Not you!"

"Okay, whatever," Roman said, quickly deciding this wasn't a fight worth having. "I'm just saying, you were never in any danger tonight. I was there to protect you."

Jessie glared at Roman for long moments. Finally she asked, "What did you tell Amir?"

"I told him he could look. He could touch your tits. But he couldn't fuck you. Your pussy was off-limits."

Jessie crossed her arms, like she was hugging herself.

Roman moved close. He wrapped his arms around her. She didn't try to pull away. "Now come on," he gently said. "Come back to bed."

Jessie looked up at him. Roman kissed her. And she didn't try pulling away.

———◉———

They kissed and fondled, and Jessie used her mouth and hands to help Roman get hard again.

Their sex went over an hour. Roman lasted even longer than usual since he had just cum. By the time they were done, their bodies glistened with sweat.

Sometimes it was lovemaking. They kissed or looked into each other's eyes, as Roman moved slowly in and out of her.

Other times it was fucking, with Jessie's legs on Roman's shoulders, or on her hands and knees, with Roman violently and relentlessly pounding her long and hard.

Roman toyed with Jessie again, not letting her cum. He found that denying her release got him hot.

Tears rolled down her face as Jessie went out of her mind with the need for an orgasm. She pleaded with him, begged him to let her cum. Roman liked when Jessie begged. That got him hot too.

Then, at last, Roman used his wonderful and talented cock to send her over the edge and into a shuddering climax that sent thunderbolts of orgasmic pleasure shooting through her lithe body. After cumming, Jessie couldn't move. She couldn't think. She couldn't talk. She could barely breathe.

It wasn't always this way, their sex. But sometimes, like tonight, Jessie's orgasms on Roman's cock were practically life altering experiences.

And during these times, the emotions Jessie felt for Roman were enormous. It was impossible not to have intense emotions for a man who gave her such physical pleasure. Sometimes, in those moments just after cumming, as she still panted and her body tingled with the after-shocks of her orgasm, she couldn't help feeling love for Roman.

Those moments scared her. And she felt guilty, feeling like she was betraying her husband.

She told herself, *feeling love for* Roman was different from *loving* Roman. The only man she loved was Ollie. Still, Jessie felt guilty.

They fell asleep in each other's arms. Late at night, Jessie slowly awoke to Roman's lips on hers. He'd been working her sleeping body and she was on fire. She realized his cock was already inside her. They made slow love, kissing and hugging as Roman slowly moved in and out, the moonlight illuminating the room. She had no idea if Roman was wearing a condom. At that moment, she didn't care. Even though she knew she was ovulating. She didn't care.

When Jessie awoke the next morning, her body ached from all the sex the night before. Her pussy ached in particular. Roman's cock had ravaged her pussy!

Jessie looked at the clock. God, she was late for work!

Roman tried to pull her back into bed. "Roman I'm late for work," she told him. She sounded half panicked.

"Call in sick," Roman flippantly said. He was still half asleep.

"I've got meetings today," Jessie said, quickly dressing as she spoke. "My boss will be furious if I miss them."

"Get a new boss," Roman said sleepily.

Jessie pushed Roman's arm to wake up. "You have to drive me home," she said. "I can't go to work looking like this." She wore the dress from last night. It was too tight and short for work. And it was wrinkled and had stains of sex. No way she could wear the dress to work.

"Okay, yeah," Roman said, finally dragging himself out of bed.

As they drove, Jessie asked "Did you wear a condom last night?"

"Yes Jessie I wore a condom," Roman said wearily. "You know, Amir came on your pussy last night. Maybe when I fucked you – *with a condom*—I pushed his sperm into you. Wouldn't it be a laugh if you've pregnant with his baby? A half Arab baby? At least with me the baby would be white."

"God Romes," Jessie lamented as she shook her head. It would be the most horrible thing in the world. If Romes got her pregnant, she and Ollie could at least pretend it was his. But if the baby's skin was as dark as Amir's? It would ruin their lives.

"You should get a new job," Roman said a few minutes later.

"My job is fine."

"You hate your job."

"Everyone hates their job," Jessie said. "The money's decent and the people are nice. The work's kind of easy. I just have to be there when my boss says I have to be there."

"Sounds kind of soul crushing," Roman said.

"Well, thanks Mr. Sunshine," Jessie joked with a laugh. "Are you always this miserable in the morning?"

"Only before coffee," Roman joked back, and they both laughed.

"So when can I see you again?" Roman asked. "I get to see you two more times this week."

"You know, it won't always be 3 times a week," Jessie said. "It kind of depends on what's going on with my life. And with your life."

"I know that," Roman said with a shrug. "So when? Tonight?"

"I'm too sore for another go with you tonight, Mister," Jessie said.

"So what? I've got a tongue," Roman said. "And you've got a mouth."

"Oh my god ...," Jessie said with a half laugh. "I need sleep too you know."

"Maybe tomorrow," she said. "And then maybe this weekend, so Ollie can be there."

"Okay," Roman agreed with a shrug. He knew there was only so far he could push.

"But can we have some, you know, normal *I'm fucking another man because my husband wants me to* kind of sex? The last times have been intense."

Roman laughed. "Okay. I'll check my *the best ways to fuck a married girl* notes," he joked.

"Make sure it's the *while the husband watches* chapter," Jessie joked back. They both laughed.

CHAPTER 11

Things continued for a couple months. Usually, Jessie went out with Roman two times a week, while Ollie was traveling. She slept over with him, usually at his house, and he drove her home in the morning. During these dates, when Jessie was alone with Roman, she wore the wig with short black hair. And she wore heavier, darker makeup. She started thinking of it as her "Roman's girlfriend" persona.

On the weekend when Ollie was home – usually Saturday night – all three went out together. On these nights, Jessie was with Roman, and Ollie was the third wheel. On these nights though, Jessie didn't wear the wig, because she knew Ollie hated seeing her in short dark hair. And she did her makeup the way she normally did with Ollie. This was her "Ollie's wife" persona.

On these nights, it pained Ollie to see Jessie wearing her wedding ring on her right hand, and Roman's #44 football ring on the ring finger of her left hand. But as always, the jealousy and angst were gasoline to the white hot flames of his cuckold desires, and looking at the rings on his wife's hands never failed to get him hard in his pants.

Fortunately, Jessie had not been late with her period. She had avoided getting pregnant. So far. Jessie and Ollie talked about it, and they agreed she would stay off the pill and not use any other birth control. This was recommended by her gynecologist anyway, although for health reasons (to allow Jessie's body to reset).

By this point, Jessie and Ollie both understood how risk added extra, delicious spice to their game. Like the risk of Roman getting Jessie pregnant. The risk of Jessie growing too close to Roman. The risk of people finding out that Jessie was having an affair with Roman.

All this risk and danger made everything more exciting, and they were becoming addicted to the thrilling highs. It was better than any drug.

Ollie hated that Jessie had a pet name for Roman – Romes. But that seemed to add a thrill to their game too.

One day while Ollie was traveling, Roman called and asked Jessie out on a date. This had become normal, and she looked forward to her dates with Roman. And to her evenings with him.

Jessie wondered if her pussy was stretching from fucking Roman so much. She knew it was becoming easier for her to take her lover's – her *boyfriend's* – long thick cock into her. Ollie often said *"you're so loose, he's stretching you out"* when they had sex. She knew the idea both horrified and thrilled her husband. And usually, Jessie would tease Ollie by saying, *"yeah baby, Romes is ruining my pussy for your little cock."*

On this particular day, Roman promised Jessie this would be a special date. She shivered at the thought. Roman had toned it down since that time in the cab with Amir. So on this *special* date, she expected the worst. She spent the afternoon emotionally preparing herself for what might happen.

About an hour before picking her up, Roman texted to Jessie: "Don't wear the wig." That surprised her. But she did as he said, wearing her long blonde hair down. And, she did her makeup the way she normally did in her "Ollie's wife" persona. Lighter colors, lighter application.

Looking into the mirror, Jessie saw the same person she'd been months ago. She *was* the same person. Wasn't she?

She still had a husband who she loved. But now, she had a boyfriend too, who she liked a lot.

A lot.

And sometimes while having sex or right after, she even felt love for Roman.

Looking into the mirror with her long blonde hair down, she looked like the same person. But she knew she wasn't.

The taxi drove them to Theater Row on West 42nd street. Jessie knew the off-Broadway and off-off-Broadway theaters were concentrated here, between 9th and 10th Avenues.

"Are we seeing a show?" Jessie asked.

Roman shook his head. "I want you to meet someone," he said.

Roman brought her into the *Duke Theater*. Inside, the cast was rehearsing a new musical. A big, well-dressed man saw them enter and waved. He motioned for them to meet in the lobby.

The man was almost as big as Roman. He was blonde and fair compared to Roman's dark hair and dark complexion.

"Jessie, this is Hammer Malone," Roman said. "My quarterback friend from Penn State."

"Oh yeah, hi," Jessie said. She was instantly embarrassed and blushed. Had he seen the videos of her getting fucked at his apartment in the HL23?

If Hammer had seen them, he didn't mention it. "They call me Hammer because I was a running quarterback," Hammer explained. With a laugh, he added "You know, running like a hammer into a brick wall of linebackers. That was me."

"I'm a big Penn State football fan. I went there. I remember you," Jessie said. "You were really awesome."

"Well, thank you, young lady for being such a polite liar," Hammer said with a modest bow, and they all laughed.

"Anyway, the NFL was stupid enough to draft me. I made some money and did pretty good investing," Hammer said. "I'm a producer now. I produce Broadway musicals."

"Oh," Jessie said. She was incredibly impressed. "That's amazing! You're so lucky!"

Hammer gave her an appreciative smile. "Roman says you're a dancer," he said. "How would you like a part in my new musical?" As he said this, he motioned to the rehearsal continuing on the stage.

Jessie's jaw dropped. She was shocked. "What? Just like that? Without auditioning?"

"We need someone now," Hammer explained. "We open in two weeks. And the other girl broke her leg. Nothing to do with my show. She slipped in the shower. Shit happens."

"I still can't believe you're offering me a part in a musical," Jessie said looking awestruck. "You don't know me."

"I spoke to your agent. He vouches for you," Hammer said. "And I won't bullshit you. It's a small part. No speaking lines. But you do get to dance as part of our dance troupe, and the dancing's in almost every scene."

"You never know," Hammer continued. "You're pretty. Prettier than Roman described, if you don't mind me saying. If the right people see you in this musical, it can lead to bigger things. It might lead to bigger things in my next musical, if you do well. You know how it works. A lot of famous actors got their start through a lucky break. Well Jessie – this is your lucky break."

Hammer said, "Anyway, think about it. But I need an answer tomorrow. Sorry for the rush, but we open in two weeks. I need you on the stage ASAP so you can learn the routines."

Jessie's head was spinning. This was all happening so fast. She had to talk to Ollie.

"I'll let you know," she promised.

Hammer nodded. Then, almost as an afterthought, he said, "You'll have to change your hair."

"My hair?" Jessie asked, not understanding.

"The dancers all need to look the same," Hammer said. "Same height, same body type. And same hair."

Hammer handed a large 8 x 10 photo to Jessie. It was a group shot of the dance troupe.

All the girls were her height. They were all slim, with small breasts, and long legs, just like Jessie.

And all the girls had short, dark hair.

"Can I wear a wig?" Jessie whispered, her throat suddenly dry and the words coming out like a mouse's squeak.

Hammer shook his head. A definitive no. "Sorry. Some of the routines are intense. Can't risk a wig falling off."

Jessie slowly nodded to Hammer. Then she looked at Roman. He was grinning.

———⊙———

Ollie, of course, canceled the rest of his business trip and rushed home. That evening, he and Jessie were sitting in their TV room. Roman wasn't there.

Ollie held the 8 x 10 photo in his hands. The girls in the dance troupe were all young, leggy, and almost flat chested. Just like Jessie.

All the girls were pretty, but Jessie would be the prettiest as soon as she joined the troupe.

Ollie looked at Jessie. His wife had long blonde hair. Natural blonde. Thick and luxurious. With a natural wave, flowing off her shoulders and extending just past her bra strap. What he liked to call *bra strap length*.

Then he looked back at the photo. The dancers all had short hair. Very short, just past their ears. And their hair was dark brown.

To take this part, Jessie would have to cut off most of her beautiful blonde hair. And then dye what remained dark brown.

The idea made Ollie hurt inside. Really, *really* hurt inside.

And the fact Roman was getting what he wanted – transforming his wife from a blonde to a brunette. It devastated him. It cut at his ego and manhood.

But Ollie never hesitated. Not even a micro-second. This was Jessie. The person he loved more than life. *It was Jessie.* And this was her dream.

Ollie forced a smile and said, "This is your big chance, Jessie. You've dreamed about this forever. You have to take this part."

"But my hair. You love my hair. I love my hair," Jessie said, undecided.

"It'll grow back," Ollie said encouragingly. "And when it comes back, it'll be blonde, just like how it is now. But then, you'll be a Broadway performer. You'll have a resume. You'll be able to get parts easier."

"I'll have to quit my job," Jessie said. "And his gig pays shit."

"It's okay. I'll be able to cover us," Ollie promised. He smiled at her again. "Don't worry. I want you to do this. I do. I love you. And this is your dream. I want you to do this."

Jessie took Ollie's hands in hers. "This is why I love you so much," she said, looking into his eyes. "This is why I will always love you."

⸺⸺⸺◉⸺⸺⸺

The next morning, Jessie called Hammer and told him she wanted the part.

Hammer seemed ambivalent about her decision. It was clear to Jessie that he didn't care if she took the part or not. This was NYC, where dancers were a dime a dozen. He could have filled this part in a second from dozens of b-grade dancers with better resumes than Jessie. The only reason he offered Jessie this part was because of his friendship with Roman.

Jessie was okay with that though. Her dream was to dance on Broadway. All she ever wanted was a chance.

Hammer gave Jessie the address of a hair salon. He said he used this salon for all his productions. They would know how to cut and dye Jessie's hair so it was perfect for the musical.

Ollie went with Jessie. He didn't want to, but he had to.

He watched as the stylist cut his wife's hair. Hacked her hair off was more like it.

Before, her hair was halfway down her back. When the stylist was done, her hair was barely past her ears. Seeing the lush locks of her hair falling to the floor, it made him want to cry.

But the stylist wasn't done. Jessie's hair was lush and thick. That wouldn't do for the troupe. The stylist severely thinned her hair to remove its lushness and natural waviness. More of Jessie's hair fell to the floor.

Then the stylist bleached Jessie's remaining hair so it was stark white. Stark white!

Her beautiful, natural blonde hair was now bright white. Again, Ollie wanted to cry.

Finally, the stylist dyed Jessie hair dark brown with dark reddish accents.

When it was all done, Ollie looked at her. He barely recognized his wife. She was no longer a long haired blonde. She was a brunette with hair that barely reached her ears.

"Are you okay Ollie?" Jessie gently asked.

Ollie forced a brave face and smiled. "You look beautiful baby," he said. She did look beautiful. But she didn't look like his wife. She looked like one of Roman's girlfriends. Like Alisha. Like one of those girls in his pictures.

Ollie and Jessie went home, and he took her to bed. He knew she was seeing Roman later. It was their date night.

Ollie wanted her first. He got on his knees. He pulled off her jeans and panties. He took off her sneakers. Jessie still had on cute white ankle socks, with a little lace fringe across the top. He left them on. He liked seeing Jessie naked except for cute little socks on her pretty feet. It was one of the many things that got him hot about his wife.

Ollie looked at her pussy, and he ran a finger along her slit. She was a little moist. Was it possible? Cutting and dying her hair, had that aroused her? Or maybe doing it for Roman, that aroused her?

Ollie looked up at Jessie's face. She was looking at him looking at her. He tried to read her pretty face but he wasn't able to. And he didn't have the courage to ask her. There was only so much he could take, and hearing her answer might tear him apart even more.

Ollie lowered his head and began eating her out. He was always able to get Jessie off with his tongue. And he wanted to make her cum. It didn't take long – it never took long when he went down on her. Soon Jessie was moaning and writhing as she orgasmed on his tongue.

After recovering, Jessie undressed Ollie and moved him to his back on their bed. They looked into each other's faces as she undressed the rest of the way, taking off her blouse and then her bra. She was naked now like Ollie, except she still wore the cute little ankle socks.

Jessie lay next to Ollie, and they hugged and kissed. They made out a while, their arms around each other, and it felt so good to Ollie. Both physically and emotionally. *He needed this.*

Jessie reached a hand down to Ollie's legs. She slowly and lightly scraped her sweet pink nails down the inside of his thighs. Ollie loved this. He moaned at the sensations, getting harder if that was even possible.

Jessie rested her head on Ollie's shoulder as she caressed his inner thighs. Then she moved her foot up to his calf. Still lightly scraping her nails along his inner thighs, she ran her foot in the cute white sock along his calf. "You like this baby?" she asked.

"Oh god Jessie it feels so good," Ollie groaned.

"You're my hero baby," Jessie told him. "Just so you know. You're my hero."

Ollie stared at Jessie as, inside, he choked up with emotions.

Jessie moved her hand to Ollie's shaft. She slowly stroked him up and down.

"This is a terrible thing to ask," she said. "But you know I'm seeing Roman later? And, you know ..."

Her voice trailed off.

"What?" Ollie asked. "Tell me."

"Would it be okay if you wore a condom?" Jessie finally asked.

Ollie stared at his wife. It was Roman's 24 hour rule.

But still ... after cutting her hair. Dying her hair. After he even agreed to their date night tonight. She was going to make him wear a condom?

Eventually Ollie nodded. Jessie gave him a weak smile, then she reached for a condom from the bedside cabinet. She tore open the small square package, then rolled the latex onto her husband's hard cock.

Then Jessie straddled Ollie's hips. She held his now sheathed cock in her hand, and guided it into her pussy. They made slow love with Jessie on top. But even as Jessie kissed him, Ollie couldn't help wondering if she was thinking about Roman.

———◉———

JESSIE AND OLLIE'S STORY CONCLUDES IN
Opening Pandora's Box
Book Five: How Could You Do That To Me?

———◉———

Available at Amazon Kindle and Smashwords.

ACKNOWLEDGEMENTS

Just a couple of short notes.

The Highline is a great public park in New York City. And the Highline 23 (HL23) is real. In fact, unit 6 is on sale now as I write this for just over $4.5 million. Apologies to the new owners for the sexy scene in their apartment. Hopefully that big window overlooking the Highline will be Windexed before they move in.

Bond 45 is a great place to go for drinks before seeing a Broadway show. Jessie and Ollie try to see shows as much as possible, but they usually chase after day-of tickets to save money.

Finally, the warm chocolate chip cookies at Culture Expresso are amazing.

Don't miss out!

Visit the website below and you can sign up to receive emails whenever Pete Andrews publishes a new book. There's no charge and no obligation.

https://books2read.com/r/B-A-KWSAB-YIVOC

BOOKS 2 READ

Connecting independent readers to independent writers.

OPENING PANDORA'S BOX

---•---

BOOK FOUR: JESSIE LOSES HERSELF IN ROMAN

---•---

PETE ANDREWS